OPEN CITY

New York City, Summer 2003
Number Seventeen

OPEN CITY

Actual Air
Poems by David Berman

"David Berman's poems are beautiful,
strange, intelligent, and funny. They are
narratives that freeze life in impossible
contortions. They take the familiar and
make it new, so new the reader is
stunned and will not soon forget. I
found much to savor on every page
of *Actual Air*. It's a book for everyone."
   —James Tate

"This is the voice I have been waiting so
long to hear . . . Any reader who tunes
in to his snappy, offbeat meditations is
in for a steady infusion of surprises and
delights."
   —Billy Collins

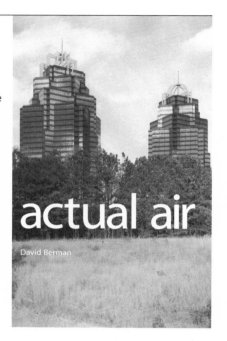

My Misspent Youth
Essays by Meghan Daum

"An empathic reporter and a provacative
autobiographer . . . I finished it in a single
afternoon, mesmerized and sputtering."
   —*The Nation*

"Essay lovers take heart. There's a new
voice on the fray, and it belongs to a
talented young writer. In this collection
of on-target analyses of American cul-
ture, Daum offers the disapproval of
youth, leavened with pithy humor and
harsh self-appraisal. . . . An edgy read."
   —*Publishers Weekly* (starred review)

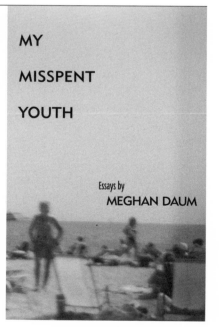

BOOKS

Venus Drive
Stories by Sam Lipsyte

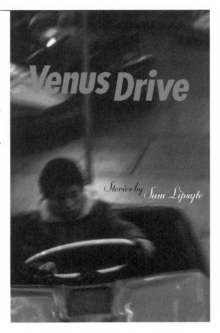

"A wickedly gifted writer. *Venus Drive* is
filled with grimly satisfying fractured
insights and hardcore humor. But it also
displays some inspired sympathy for the
daze and confusion of its characters . . .
wonderfully written and compulsively
readable with brilliant and funny dialog,
a collection that represents the emer-
gence of a very strong talent."
   —Robert Stone

"Sam Lipsyte can get blood out of a
stone—rich, red human blood from the
stony sterility of contemporary life . . . I
gripped this book so hard my knuckles
turned white."
   —Edmund White

World on Fire
by Michael Brownstein

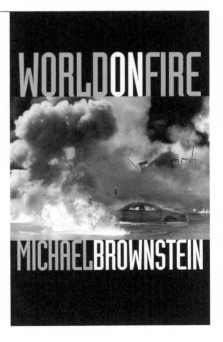

"Bold and ambitious, *World on Fire*
engages the great issues of the day,
mixing the personal with the political,
demanding attention be paid, continuing in the great tradition of Whitman,
Ginsberg, and Pound. Here's a howl
for the twenty-first century."
   —Eric Schlosser, author of
   Fast Food Nation

"One of the most eloquent recent poetic
works to cover the downsides of 'progress'
and to cry out for a counterpunch against
the manipulations of empire."
   —*Publishers Weekly* (starred review)

OPEN CITY

CONTRIBUTORS' NOTES 12

CHUCK KINDER 31 The Girl with No Face

MARK JUDE POIRIER 39 Happy Pills

JASON FOX 51 Models and Monsters

SAÏD SAYRAFIEZADEH 59 My Mother and the Stranger

WILLIAM BOWERS 67 It Takes a Nation of Millions to Hold Us Back

CYNTHIA WEINER 71 Amends

CHRISTOPH HEEMANN 91 Pencil Drawings

JACK FITZGERALD 99 A Drop in the Bucket

HONOR MOORE 105 In Place of an Introduction

TWENTY-FIVE POETS 107 Special Poetry Section

JESSICA LAMB-SHAPIRO 167 The Man Is Eating in His Sleep

STU MEAD 177 Devil Milk

RICK DeMARINIS 185 The Life and Times of a Forty-Nine Pound Man

JESSE GOLDSTEIN 197 Dance with Me Ish, Like When You Was a Baby

SOPHIE TOULOUSE 201 Sexy Clowns

GREG AMES 209 Physical Discipline

MARCEL COHEN 217 *From* Letter to Antonio Saura

BRUNO SCHLEINSTEIN 227 Drawings

MARCELLE CLEMENTS 239 Reliable Alchemy

LARA VAPYNAR 243 There Are Jews in My House

BUZZER THIRTY THANKS THE ARTISTS, WRITERS & EDUCATORS OF OUR FIRST YEAR

REBECCA GODFREY	ROBERT CARLUCCI	MICHAEL LEONG
ERIKA deVRIES	RACHEL SHERMAN	WADE NACINOVICH
JOHN BROUGHTON	MONICA GOETZ	HELEN KLEIN ROSS
KRISTA McGRUDER	AMY BAY	MARC WOODWORTH
LIVIA ALEXANDER	SIAN FOLKES	NAOMI LEIMSIDER
AARON BEEBE	JAMES EARL HARDY	HANNAH TINTI
ED SIKOV	CHRIS PRENTICE	CHRIS CHANIN
LEE ANN BROWN	THOMAS GLAVE	KARL KIRCHWEY
SAM LIPSYTE	DARIN STRAUSS	SHELLEY JACKSON

BUZZER THIRTY

WWW.BUZZERTHIRTY.COM
38-01 23RD AVE
ASTORIA, NY 11105

A WRITING AND ARTS EDUCATION CENTER

STEPHEN MALKMUS
& THE JICKS

PIG LIB

LP/CD
In Stores Now

OPEN CITY

Open City is published triannually by Open City, Inc., a not-for-profit corporation. Donations are tax-deductible to the extent allowed by the law. A one-year subscription (3 issues) is $30; a two-year subscription (6 issues) is $55. Make checks payable to: Open City, Inc., 270 Lafayette Street, Suite 1412, New York, NY 10012. For credit-card orders, see our Web site: www.opencity.org. E-mail: editors@opencity.org.

Front cover by Stu Mead, *Untitled*, acrylic on canvas, 2002.
Back cover by Lori Ellison.
Front page drawing by Jason Fox.

Open City gratefully acknowledges the generous support of the Family of Robert Bingham. We also thank The Greenwall Foundation, the New York State Council on the Arts, and the National Endowment for the Arts.

State of the Arts

NYSCA

NATIONAL
ENDOWMENT
FOR THE ARTS

ISBN 1-890447-31-5
ISSN 1089-5523

OPEN CITY

EDITORS
Thomas Beller
Joanna Yas

ART DIRECTOR
Nick Stone

EDITORS-AT-LARGE
Adrian Dannatt
Elizabeth Schmidt

ASSISTANT EDITOR
Alicia Bergman

CONTRIBUTING EDITORS
Lee Ann Brown
Sam Brumbaugh
Vanessa Chase
Amanda Gersh
Laura Hoffmann
Kip Kotzen
Anthony Lacavaro
Alix Lambert
Sam Lipsyte
Jim Merlis
Honor Moore
Parker Posey
Alexandra Tager
Tony Torn
Lee Smith
Jocko Weyland

READERS
Twilight Greenaway
Jessica Hoffmann
Nadxieli Mannello

FOUNDING EDITORS
Thomas Beller
Daniel Pinchbeck

FOUNDING PUBLISHER
Robert Bingham

CONTRIBUTORS' NOTES

AMMIEL ALCALAY's poetry, prose, reviews, critical articles, and translations have appeared in *The New York Times Book Review*, *The New Yorker*, *The New Republic*, *Grand Street*, *Conjunctions*, *The Nation*, and various other publications. His books include *Memories of Our Future: Selected Essays* and *After Jews and Arabs: Remaking Levantine Culure*.

GREG AMES lives in Brooklyn. His stories have appeared in *Fiction International*, *The Sun*, *McSweeney's*, *Literal Latte*, and *Other Voices*.

JILL BIALOSKY is the author of two books of poetry, *The End of Desire* and *Subterranean* (Alfred A. Knopf), and a novel, *House Under Snow* (Harcourt). She lives in New York City.

JULIA BOLUS is literary assistant to playwright Arthur Miller, academic director of Kent School Summer Writers Camp, and cofounder of Digital Dream Multimedia. She also works as an archivist and researcher. A play based on her most recent collection of poems, *Circus of Infinite Attractions*, premiered at the 2001 New York International Fringe Festival. Selected poems and more about the book/theater piece can be found on her site, www.circusplay.com.

WILLIAM BOWERS is a South Carolinian in Florida. He has written about music for *The Oxford American*, *Magnet*, *No Depression*, and Pitchforkmedia.com. He went through a phase of publishing poems in small places, such as *The Wallace Stevens Journal* and *Sonora Review*. A book is forthcoming from Harcourt.

PEG BOYERS is executive editor of *Salmagundi* magazine. She is most recently the author of *Hard Bread*, a book of poems.

MARCELLE CLEMENTS's novel, *Midsummer*, from which "Reliable Alchemy" is an outtake, was published in May by Harcourt. Her previous books include *The Dog Is Us,* a collection of essays, and *Rock Me*, a novel.

MARCEL COHEN's most recent book is *Faits: Lectures courante à l'usage des grands débutants* (Gallimard, 2002). Two of his earlier books have been translated into English, *Mirrors* (Green Integer, 1998) and *The Emperor Peacock Moth* (Burning Deck, 1995).

RICK DeMARINIS is the author of seven novels, including *A Clod of Wayward Marl*, his latest; five collections of short stories; and *The Art and Craft of the Short Story*. His stories have appeared in *Esquire*, *The Atlantic*, *GQ*, and many literary quarterlies. In 1990, he won a literature award from the American Academy of Arts and Letters, and his collection, *Borrowed Time: New and Selected Stories*, won the 1999 Independent Book Publishers Award for best book of short fiction. He lives in Missoula, Montana.

LORI ELLISON is the Mary Poppins of Tribeca.

DANIEL MARK EPSTEIN is the author of seven books of poetry, in print at Liveright/Norton and Overlook/Viking, most recently, *The Traveler's Calendar*. His poems have appeared in *The New Yorker*, *The Atlantic Monthly*, *The Paris Review*, and other magazines. He is also the author of biographies of Nat King Cole and Edna St. Vincent Millay. He has won a Guggenheim Fellowship, and the Prix de Rome from the American Academy of Arts and Letters.

JACK FITZGERALD grew up in southern Vermont, and for the time being he resides in Brooklyn, New York. This is his first published story.

JASON FOX is an artist who lives in Poughkeepsie, New York. He is represented by Feature Inc. in New York City.

CAROLYN FORCHÉ's new collection *Blue Hour* was published this spring by HarperCollins. Her previous collections are *The Angel of History*, *The Country Between Us*, and *Gathering the Tribes*. She lives in Washington, D.C., and teaches in the graduate writing program at George Mason University.

PETER GIZZI's latest book is *Artificial Heart*. He has two new limited-edition chapbooks: *Revival* with artwork by David Byrne and *Fin Amore* with artwork by George Herms. His new book, *Some Values of Landscape and Weather*, is forthcoming from Wesleyan University Press in fall 2003.

JESSE GOLDSTEIN shares his birthday with Barry Hannah and lives off the most beautiful train in Brooklyn. This is his first published story.

EAMON GRENNAN is from Dublin and teaches at Vassar College, where he is the Dexter M. Ferry, Jr. Professor of English. He has also taught recently at Villanova University, New York University, and Columbia University. His most recent collections are *Relations: New & Selected Poems* and *Still Life with Waterfall*.

TOM HEALY owned one of the first contemporary art galleries in Chelsea. He is now president of Creative Time. His poems have appeared in *The Paris Review*, *Tin House*, *Salmagundi*, *LIT*, *Drunken Boat* and the anthologies *Tigertail* and *Aroused*. He lives in New York and Miami.

CHRISTOPH HEEMANN lives in Germany where he was born in 1964. Since 1983 he has worked on music with various projects and individuals (Mirror, Mimir, Jim O'Rourke, Current 93, Keiji Haino, et cetera) and has also recorded albums under his own name. He operates the Streamline label and has enjoyed graphic work ever since he can remember.

CYNTHIA MARIE HOFFMAN is a teaching fellow in the MFA poetry program at George Mason University. She is the founding editor of *Frantic Egg: A Mini-Journal of Poetry*, and she is a member of the editorial board at the Word Works. Her publications include the journals *Rattapallax*, *Phoebe*, and *Heliotrope*, and her awards include the Mary Roberts Rinehart Award, the Virginia Downs Poetry Award, and a scholarship to attend a poetry workshop in St. Petersburg, Russia.

FANNY HOWE's book of poems, *Gone*, was published this spring, and a collection of essays, *The Wedding Dress*, will be published this fall, both by University of California Press.

SUJI KWOCK KIM's first book, *Notes from the Divided Country*, won the 2002 Whitman Award of the Academy of American Poets, selected by Yusef Komunyakaa, and was published by Louisiana State University Press in April. Her poems and translations have appeared in *The Nation*, *The New Republic*, *The Paris Review*, *Poetry*, *The Yale Review*, *DoubleTake*, *Threepenny Review*, *Tin House*, and other journals. Currently she is assistant professor of English at Drew University.

CHUCK KINDER's most recent novel is *Honeymooners: A Cautionary Tale*. "The Girl With No Face" is a chapter from his forthcoming metamemoir, *The Last Mountain Dancer*. He is the director of the writing program at the University of Pittsburgh.

JOANNA KLINK's first book of poems, *They Are Sleeping*, was recently published by the University of Georgia Press. She teaches in the M.F.A. program at the University of Montana.

JESSICA LAMB-SHAPIRO, a founding member of the New Politeness, is a student in the M.F.A. program at Columbia University. This is her first publication.

JOAN LARKIN's poetry collections are *Housework*, *A Long Sound*, *Sor Juana's Love Poems* (co-translated with Jaime Manrique), and *Cold River*. *The Living*, her play about AIDS, was produced at the Brooklyn Arts Exchange. She teaches poetry writing at Sarah Lawrence and New England College.

ELIZABETH MACKLIN has published two collections of poems, *A Woman Kneeling in the Big City* and *You've Just Been Told*. In 1999–2000 she spent an Amy Lowell Poetry Traveling Scholarship year studying the Basque language in Bilbao, Spain. She lives in New York City.

DONNA MASINI's books include *That Kind of Danger* (Beacon Press) and the novel, *About Yvonne*, (W. W. Norton). A recipient of NEA and NYFA grants, her poems have appeared in *TriQuarterly*, *The Paris Review*, *Parnassus*, *Boulevard*, and others. She is a professor of English at Hunter College. Her new collection of poems, *Turning to Fiction*, is forthcoming from W. W. Norton.

RICHARD MATTHEWS is the author of *The Mill Is Burning* (Grove Press, 2002). He lives in New York City.

STU MEAD lives in Berlin and exhibits his work at Endart, Berlin. From 1991–1997 he collaborated with Frank Gaard on a zine called *Manbag*, which is available as a compilation published by le Dernier Cri, Marseille. His new book, *Miniput*, will come out this year, also from le Dernier Cri.

SEMEZDIN MEHMEDINOVIC was born in Bosnia in 1960, and was educated at the University of Sarajevo. In 1994, with five other Bosnian writers, he received the Hellman-Hammet Award from PEN for persistence in preserving democracy in the midst of war. Mehmedinovic arrived in the United States as a political refugee in 1996, and he is currently living in Alexandria, Virginia. His books include *Sarajevo Blues* (1998) and *Nine Alexandrias*, forthcoming next fall; both are from City Lights and translated from the Bosnian by Ammiel Alcalay.

JANE MILLER's book-length poem, *A Palace of Pearls*, will be out in 2004 from Copper Canyon Press.

HONOR MOORE is the guest poetry editor for this issue. Her most recent collection of poems is *Darling* (Grove Press, 2001).

EILEEN MYLES is a poet who lives in New York and a novelist who teaches fiction at UCSD. She is working on a libretto called *Hell* and a novel called *The Inferno*.

Poet and translator **G. E. PATTERSON**'s first book, *Tug*, is available from Graywolf Press. Recent work can be found in *American Letters and Commentary*, *Five Fingers Review*, *Swerve*, *XCP*, and *Seneca Review*.

MARK JUDE POIRIER is the author of two collections of short stories, *Unsung Heroes of American Industry* and *Naked Pueblo*; and the novel, *Goats*. He's currently on the literature faculty at Bennington College in Vermont.

ROBERT POLITO is the author of the poetry collection, *Doubles* (Chicago), *A Reader's Guide to James Merrill's The Changing Light at Sandover* (Michigan), and *Savage Art: A Biography of Jim Thompson* (Knopf/Vintage), which received the National Book Critics Circle Award. He is editing a book of Manny Farber's film and art criticism, and completing a new book of poems. He directs the graduate writing program at The New School.

VICTORIA REDEL's most recent book is the novel *Loverboy*. Her collection of poems, *Swoon*, is forthcoming from University of Chicago Press. She currently teaches at Sarah Lawrence and Columbia University.

RAPHAEL RUBINSTEIN's books include *The Basement of the Café Rilke* (1997), *Postcards from Alphaville* (2000) and the forthcoming *Polychrome Profusion: Selected Art Criticism 1990–2002*, all published by Hard Press. In 2002, the French government named him a Chevalier dans l'Ordre des Art et des Lettres.

SAÏD SAYRAFIEZADEH's essay, "Reflections of a Savage," appeared in the anthology, *Before and After: Stories from New York*. He is currently at work on a playwrighting commission from New York Theatre Workshop about the New York City draft riots of 1863. He lives and works in New York City and is terrified of cockroaches.

BRUNO SCHLEINSTEIN was born in 1932 as the illegitimate child of a German father and a Polish mother. He was brought up in orphanages and in institutions for the mentally ill. In 1955, he was released after several escapes. Living in Berlin in the sixties, working as a forklift operator, he began to play the accordion and illustrate his songs with drawings. In 1974, he starred as Kaspar Hauser in Werner Herzog's film *Every Man for Himself and God Against All*; two years later he acted in another Herzog film, *Stroszek*. The filmmaker Miron Zwonir recently released a documentary about Bruno S.'s life entitled *Estrangement Is Death*.

SOPHIE TOULOUSE is a visual artist. She lives and works in New York City and spends summers on Nation of Angela Island. To learn more, go to www.nationofangela.com

KIRMEN URIBE is the author of *Bitartean heldu eskutik* (Meanwhile Hold Hands), which won Spain's 2001 Premio de la Crítica, and, with the musician Mikel Urdangarin, *Bar Puerto*, a CD-book. He makes his living as a scriptwriter for Basque public television and lives in Vitoria-Gasteiz (Euskadi).

LARA VAPNYAR came to New York from Moscow in 1994. Her short-story collection, *There Are Jews in My House*, will be published by Pantheon this fall.

CYNTHIA WEINER teaches at the Writers Studio and Pace University in Manhattan. She is working on a collection of short stories.

SUSAN WHEELER is the author of three books of poetry, most recently *Source Codes* from Salt Publishing. The recipient of a 1999 Guggenheim Fellowship and the Witter Bynner Prize for Poetry from the American Academy of Arts and Letters in 2002, she teaches at Princeton University and is on the graduate faculty in creative writing at The New School.

C. K. WILLIAMS's most recent books of poetry are *The Vigil*; *Repair*, which won the Pulitzer Prize; and a collection of his poems on love, *Love About Love*. A book of essays, *Poetry and Consciousness*, appeared in 1998, and a book of autobiographical meditation, *Misgivings*, in 2000; it received the PEN Martha Albrand Memoir Award. He has recently completed a play, *Operations*. His new book of poems, *The Singing*, will be published in the fall of 2003. He teaches in the writing program at Princeton University.

ELIZABETH WILLIS's third book of poetry, *Turneresque*, is forthcoming from Burning Deck this spring. Her second collection, *The Human Abstract*, was selected for the National Poetry Series and published by Penguin in 1995. She teaches at Wesleyan University.

OPEN

Stories by Mary Gaitskill, Hubert Selby Jr., Vince Passaro. Art by Jeff Koons, Ken Schles, Devon Dikeou. (Vastly overpriced at $200, but fortunately we've had some takers. Only twelve copies left.)

ISSUE # 1

Stories by Martha McPhee, Terry Southern, David Shields, Jaime Manrique, Kip Kotzen. Art by Paul Ramirez-Jonas, Kate Milford, Richard Serra. (Ken Schles found the negative of our cover girl on Thirteenth Street and Avenue B. We're still looking for the girl. $25)

ISSUE # 2

Stories by Irvine Welsh, Richard Yates, Patrick McCabe. Art by Francesca Woodman, Jacqueline Humphries, Chip Kidd, Allen Ginsberg, Alix Lambert. Plus Alfred Chester's letters to Paul Bowles. (Our cover girl now has long brown hair. $25)

ISSUE # 3

Stories by Cyril Connolly, Thomas McGuane, Jim Thompson, Samantha Gillison, Michael Brownstein, Emily Carter. Art by Julianne Swartz and Peter Nadin. Poems by David Berman and Nick Tosches. Plus Denis Johnson in Somalia. (A monster issue, sales undercut by slightly rash choice of cover art by editors. Get it while you can! $15)

ISSUE # 4

Change or Die
Stories by David Foster Wallace, Siobhan Reagan, Irvine Welsh. Jerome Badanes' brilliant novella, "Change or Die" (film rights still available). Poems by David Berman and Vito Acconci. Plus Helen Thorpe on the murder of Ireland's most famous female journalist, and Delmore Schwartz on T. S. Eliot's squint. (Sold-out! We'll reprint if enough of you freak out.)

ISSUE # 5

CITY back issues

The Only Woman He's Ever Left

Stories by James Purdy, Jocko Weyland, Strawberry Saroyan. Michael Cunningham goes way uptown. Poems by Rick Moody, Deborah Garrison, Monica Lewinsky, Charlie Smith. Art by Matthew Ritchie, Ellen Harvey, Cindy Stefans. Rem Koolhaas project. With a beautiful cover by Adam Fuss. (Only $10 for this blockbuster.)

ISSUE #6

The Rubbed Away Girl

Stories by Mary Gaitskill, Bliss Broyard, and Sam Lipsyte. Art by Jimmy Raskin, Laura Larson, and Jeff Burton. Poems by David Berman, Elizabeth Macklin, Steve Malkmus, and Will Oldham. (Almost sold-out! See #5. $50)

ISSUE #7

Beautiful to Strangers

Stories by Caitlin O'Connor Creevy, Joyce Johnson, and Amine Wefali. Poems by Harvey Shapiro, Jeffrey Skinner, and Daniil Kharms. Art by David Robbins, Liam Gillick, and Elliott Puckette. Piotr Uklanski's cover is a panoramic view of Queens, shot from the top of the World Trade Center in 1998. ($10)

ISSUE #8

Bewitched

Stories by Jonathan Ames, Said Shirazi, and Sam Lipsyte. Essays by Geoff Dyer and Alexander Chancellor, who hates rabbit. Poems by Chan Marshall, Lucy Anderson, and Edvard Munch on intimate and sensitive subjects. Art by Karen Kilimnick, Giuseppe Penone, Mark Leckey, Maurizio Cattelan, and M.I.M.E. (Oddly enough, our bestselling issue. ($10)

ISSUE #9

Editors' Issue

Previously demure editors publish themselves. Enormous changes at the last minute. Stories by Robert Bingham, Thomas Beller, Daniel Pinchbeck, Joanna Yas, Adrian Dannatt, Kip Kotzen, Geoffrey O' Brien, Lee Smith, Amanda Gersh, and Jocko Weyland. Poems by Tony Torn. Art by Nick Stone, Meghan Gerety, and Alix Lambert. ($10)

ISSUE #10

OPEN

Octo Ate Them All
Vestal McIntyre emerges from the slush pile like aphrodite with a brilliant story that corresponds to the tattoo that covers his entire back. Siobhan Reagan thinks about strangulation. Fiction by Melissa Pritchard and Bill Broun. Anthropologist Michael Taussig's Cocaine Museum. Gregor von Rezzori's meditation on solitude, sex, and raw meat. Art by Joanna Kirk, Sebastien de Ganay, and Ena Swansea.($10)

ISSUE # 11

Equivocal Landscape
Sam Brumbaugh in Kenya, Daphne Beal and Swamiji, Paula Bomer sees red on a plane, Heather Larimer hits a dog, and Hunter Kennedy on the sexual possibilties of Charlottesville versus West Texas. Ford Madox Ford on the end of fun. Poetry by Jill Bialosky and Rachel Wetzsteon. Art by Miranda Lichtenstein and Pieter Schoolwerth; a love scene by Toru Hayashi. Mungo Thomson passes notes. ($10)

ISSUE # 12

Hi-fi
Sam Lipsyte introduces the subject, Steve. Nick Tosches smokes with God. Jack Walls remembers the gangs of Chicago. Vince Passaro ponders adult content. Poetry by Honor Moore, Sarah Gorham, and Melissa Holbrook Pierson. Mini-screenplay by Terry Southern. Art by Luisa Kazanas, Peter Pinchbeck, and Julianne Swartz. Special playwrighting section guest edited by Tony Torn. ($10)

ISSUE # 13

Something Like Ten Million
The defacto life and death issue. Amazing debut stories from Nico Baumbach, Michiko Okubo, and Sarah Porter; *Law and Order*'s Craig Chester writes on why he has the face he deserves; a bushy, funny, and phallic art project from Louise Belcourt. Special poetry section guest edited by Lee Ann Brown. A photo essay of fleeing Manhattanites by Ken Schles. The cover is beautiful and weird, a bright hole in downtown Manhattan. ($10)

ISSUE # 14

That Russian Question
Another excerpt from Amine Wefali's *Westchester Burning*, in stores now. Alicia Erian on the emotional cost of jeopardy. James Lasdun on travel and infidelity. Lara Vapnyar's debut publication. Jocko Weyland responds to the question, "When is your type going to learn your lesson?" The Answer Is Never. ($10)

ISSUE # 15

CITY back issues

I Wait, I Wait.
A brilliant outtake from Robert Bingham's *Lightning on the Sun*. Ryan Kenealy on the girl who ran off with the circus; Nick Tosches on Proust. Art by Allen Ruppersberg, David Bunn, Nina Katchadourian, Matthew Higgs, and Matthew Brannon. Stories by Evan Harris, Lewis Robinson, Michael Sledge, and Bruce Jay Friedman. Two letters from Rick Rofihe. Poetry by Dana Goodyear, Nathaniel Bellows, Kevin Young. A shockingly good issue with a cover many of us can relate to. ($10)

SUBSCRIBE

One year (3 issues) for $30; two years (6 issues) for $55 (includes a free T-shirt). Add $10/year for Canada & Mexico; $20/year for all other countries.

T-SHIRTS

Nice, black, 100% cotton T-shirts with white type, with the Open City logo on the front, and the words Always Open on the back.* Available in men's medium, large, x-large, or women's medium. Only $15!

*T-shirt concept by Jason Middlebrook.

Please send a check or money order payable to:

OPEN CITY, Inc.
270 Lafayette Street, Suite 1412, New York, NY 10012
For credit-card orders, see www.opencity.org.

Recycle-a-Bike is an environmental education
and job training program for New York City youth.

We sell refurbished bikes and do repairs
to support our mission. Visit our shops at:

75 Avenue C in Manhattan (212) 475-1655
55 Washington Street in Brooklyn (718) 858-2972
or www.recycleabicycle.org

C R O W D

ISSUE 3

WINTER/SPRING 2003

MARY JO BANG
WEI DONG
PAUL MULDOON
GEOFFREY G. O'BRIEN
COLE SWENSEN
KARA WALKER
SUSAN WHEELER
REBECCA WOLFF
and more...

NOW ACCEPTING ART, FICTION, PHOTOGRAPHY & POETRY SUBMISSIONS

For subscriptions and submissions
please write to:

CROWD magazine
487 Union Street, #3
Brooklyn NY 11231

WWW.CROWDMAGAZINE.COM

OPEN CITY
KGB READING SERIES

PAST, PRESENT, AND FUTURE READERS INCLUDE:

Betsy Andrews • Nico Baumbach • Daphne Beal • Joshua Beckman • Thomas Beller • David Berman • Jill Bialosky • Paula Bomer • Michael Brownstein • Annie Bruno • Sam Brumbaugh • Heather Byer • Bryan Charles • Craig Chester • Susan Connell-Mettauer • Tom Cushman • Adrian Dannatt • Eric Darton • Gabriel Marc Delahaye • Mary Donnelly • Dahlia Elsayed • Alicia Erian • Bruce Jay Friedman • Daniel Greene • Dana Goodyear • Elizabeth Grove • Evan Harris • Noy Holland • Mira Jacob • Ryan Kenealy • Hunter Kennedy • Suji Kwok Kim • Heather Larimer • James Lasdun • Sam Lipsyte • Nick Mamatas • Matt Marinovich • Ann Marlowe • Vestal McIntyre • Martha McPhee • Jim Merlis • Honor Moore • Carolyn Murnick • Maggie Nelson • Arthur Nersessian • Daniel Oppenheimer • Michael Panes • Vince Passaro • Daniel Pinchbeck • Sarah Porter • Greg Purcell • Andrea Reising • Rebecca Reynolds • Rick Rofihe • Matthew Rohrer • Saïd Sayrafiezadeh • John Seabrook • Eric Schlosser • Harvey Shapiro • Jeff Sharlet • Peter Nolan Smith • Sabin Streeter • Jean Strong • Toby Talbot • Nick Toshes • Jack Walls • Charles Waters • Paolina Weber • Amine Wefali • Rachel Wetzsteon • Jocko Weyland • Tim Wilson

KGB BAR IS AT 85 E. 4TH STREET, NEW YORK CITY

THE READINGS TAKE PLACE ON THE
FOURTH WEDNESDAY OF EVERY MONTH AT 7 P.M.
SEE **WWW.OPENCITY.ORG** FOR DETAILS
ON UPCOMING READERS.

EMAIL EDITORS@OPENCITY.ORG
WITH QUESTIONS.

The hard manual labor of the imagination. No harder than ditch-digging or wrestling alligators in public with your pants down. A terrible experience, during which the hair falls out and the teeth decay. The most ingenious torture ever devised for sins committed in previous lives. Laborious and unforgiving. A refuge from unhappiness, but with its own sorrows. The only socially acceptable form of schizophrenia.

editors' awards for emerging writers

Final Judge for Fiction Award: Steven Barthelme
Final Judge for Poetry Award: Kim Addonizio

$1,500 & PUBLICATION IN EACH CATEGORY

Postmark deadline: June 15, 2003
Reading fee: $15
Includes a year's subscription to Swink

All entries considered for publication.
Fiction entries should include one story, not to exceed 6,000 words.
Poetry entries should include up to 5 poems.
All entries considered anonymously.
Entrant's name should appear only on the cover letter.
No previously published pieces, or pieces forthcoming elsewhere.
Entrants should not yet have a nationally published book of fiction, creative nonfiction or poetry.
Winning selections to be published in the inaugural issue of Swink Magazine in the fall of 2003.
Include a SASE for notification of winners and finalists.

SEND ENTRIES TO:
Swink
Awards for Emerging Writers
244 Fifth Avenue #2722
New York, NY 10001

FOR COMPLETE GUIDELINES GO TO: WWW.SWINKMAG.COM/CONTESTS

GOD SAVE MY QUEEN *a tribute*
by DANIEL NESTER

ISBN: 1-887218-27-1 | Trade Paper | 140 pp. | 7x7 | $13.00 | Music/Memoir/Poetry

In *God Save My Queen* a short essay or riff accompanies, in order of album and track, every song recorded by the British rock band Queen, in chronological order. Part memoir, part prose poetry, part rock book, Nester's first book is genre bending at its poignant and hilarious best. It will, it will, rock you.

Daniel Nester's work has appeared in *Open City, Nerve, Mississippi Review,* and *The Best American Poetry 2003.* He is the editor in chief of the online literary journal *Unpleasant Event Schedule* (www.unpleasanteventschedule.com), former editor in chief of *La Petite Zine,* and contributing editor of *Painted Bride Quarterly.*

"Daniel Nester is a transcendent trickster, a Gogol of Rock 'n' Roll. This book is not, like so much contemporary literature, merely a realistic snapshot of life, but an ambitious effort to find in music the rhythms of life itself."
—Darin Strauss, author of *Chang and Eng* and *The Real McCoy*

"*God Save My Queen* is funny and sorrowful and strange, just like 'Bohemian Rhapsody' was before the buffoons stole it away, just like being young and alive was before we got old and alive. Nester has wrested it all back for us in this antic, tender book."
—Sam Lipsyte, author of *The Subject Steve* and *Venus Drive*

"Nester has invented the perfect form for his obsession—poems inseparable from the songs they replay, liner notes to a never-ending epiphany."
—David Trinidad, author of *Plasticville*

SOFT SKULL PRESS | 71 BOND ST., BROOKLYN, NY 11217 | WWW.SOFTSKULL.COM

THE SAINT ANN'S REVIEW

A Journal of Contemporary Arts & Letters

William Baer
Beth Bosworth
Mark Brazaitis
A.S. Calypso
Kristen Case
Maile Chapman
Vic Coccimiglio
Mary Crow
Eileen Cruz Coleman
Stephen Dixon
Susan Dugan
Carroll Dunham
Benjamin Gantcher
Meghan Hickey

William Hogeland
David Kowalczyk
Phillip Lopate
James Manlow
Mark McCloskey
Katherine Merz
Eitan Muller
Sara Nolan
Meghan O'Rourke
Lynn Saville
Harvey Shapiro
Hal Sirowitz
Anna Ziegler

The Saint Ann's Review
Saint Ann's School
129 Pierrepont Street
Brooklyn, New York 11201
saintannsreview.com

Volume Four, Number One
On Sale Now

LINCOLN PLAZA CINEMAS

Six Screens

63RD STREET & BROADWAY
OPPOSITE LINCOLN CENTER
212-757-2280

Night. Frozen plains. Trees seeking sunlight. All of
Europe, frigid. The cities stretched out like
old prostitutes. Cold. Shame when,
from time to time, someone
remembers   again;
shame   smothered
under the white
cotton of win-
ter. (Cohen,
page 217)

The Girl with No Face

Chuck Kinder

I DON'T KNOW HOW MANY FOLKS OUTSIDE OF WEST VIRGINIA remember Dagmar anymore, but once she was famous. Back in the early and mid-fifties, Dagmar had been black-and-white TV's version of Marilyn Monroe, or, maybe more accurately, of B movie queen Jayne Mansfield. Dagmar was the resident dumb blonde with big breasts on the old *Milton Berle Texaco Theater*, where she cultivated a funny, startled, deceptively stupid look. She also appeared on the TV variety show *Broadway Open House*, and even had her own short-lived *Dagmar's Canteen* in 1952, where Frank Sinatra was once a guest.

Dagmar had been my own first hope and inspiration for a future beyond the ordinary. She had become the source of all my earliest discovery and flight and fame fantasies. But I let Dagmar and her famous big breasts slip through my fingers.

Dagmar's real name was Virginia Ruth Egnor, and she was born in 1924 in Huntington, West Virginia. When I was a boy, Dagmar's folks had lived three doors down from us on Waverly Road in Huntington for several years. There were no fences around the small-frame houses on our road back in those days, and we kids darted in our games like free-range chickens across that little prairie of backyards. In Dagmar's folks' backyard there was a spreading old oak we often used as homebase, where I relished the role of being "it" during hide-and-seek. Being "it" meant that I could hover about that homebase old oak, where it was only a matter of time until one day Dagmar would discover me. Someday Dagmar would be visiting her folks, maybe sitting out at the kitchen table sipping coffee one morning with her Mom, when through the back window she would spot a swift, singular, beautiful boy fearless at his play, and with a mere glance Dagmar would recognize the shining of his inner star.

Dagmar would stub out the cigarette she had been languidly smoking, while trying to explain the enigmatic nature of fame to her old Mom, and she would rush out the backdoor to that special splendid boy, rush to enfold him in her fame, not to mention extraordinary bosom, her famous nipples fiery red through her filmy clinging negligee (I loved those words: *nipples, negligee, nipples, nipples, nipples*, which were among those magically learned juicy words of my childhood I would roll around on my tongue like holy cherry Life Savers.)

And then it really happened. Dagmar had actually shown up at her folks' home on Waverly Road the summer I was ten. We awakened one August Saturday morning into all the ordinariness of our own lives to discover an enormous car parked in front of Dagmar's folks' little house. It was a CADILLAC! It was a Cadillac CONVERTIBLE! It was YELLOW! I loved that car at first sight. The neighborhood was abuzz. One of Dagmar's prissy little nieces kept sashaying out of the house to preen and prance and keep everybody abreast of the radiant blonde being within. Apparently Dagmar had brought her latest husband home to meet her folks for a real low-key downhome family visit. I skulked and lurked about the little frame house like all the rest of the obscure neighborhood minions that Saturday morning hoping to get at least a peek at the inscrutable face of fame, but to no avail.

Around noon my Dad, or Captain as everybody called him, piled as many neighborhood kids as would fit in his old battered green Plymouth station wagon, as was his Saturday afternoon custom, and hauled us down the road to a public swimming pool called Dreamland. Dad was called Captain because he had been the captain of the Second World War, which he had apparently won pretty much single-handedly. He was famous for this. When he had mustered out of the army at the end of the war a hero, some folks had encouraged him to get into politics. Captain was a big, gregarious fellow with an easy booming laugh, a full-blown sort of character folks always declared was a dead ringer for John Wayne, and it was true. Some folks even declared that Captain would be a natural for governor of West Virginia, although he was by nature neither a drunk nor a crook. Captain, who was a generally unemployed hero, hauled all us rowdy kids out of the neighborhood on weekends so that my Mom, who was an emergency room night shift nurse, and who pretty much brought home the proverbial bacon in our house plus cooked it up, could collapse in peace.

I recall Dreamland as a vast pool of wavy, faintly blue-green water splashing with sunlight, air thick with the pungent puzzling sweetness of chlorine and suntan lotion, joyful screams and squeals strangely echoey, smooth oiled teenage girls parading imperiously with their movie star sunglasses and implicating smiles and the sweet shadowy secrets of their shaved underarms. Music was always blasting from a huge white-stucco two-storied clubhouse trimmed in blue, and blue onion-shaped domes rose above dressing rooms on a knoll at the far end of the long pool. Dreamland was a Taj Mahal of a swimming pool I both loved and feared, a site of excitement and profound failure for me.

Dreamland was where I learned to swim my first spastic strokes, and where I failed repeatedly to muster courage enough to attempt swimming out to the deep end. I was not afraid of drowning in the deep end. It wasn't that. It was, for one thing, my fear of not looking cool and sleek swimming around like the older boys, but dopey as a duck as I thrashed about in the water of the deep end. I was afraid of being embarrassed if I swam out to the huge circular concrete float in the deep end where the older boys hung out as they strutted and flexed their fulsome brown muscled bodies. Mostly, though, my fear of the deep end was because of the bad dreams.

We piled out of Captain's old Plymouth station wagon that Saturday and charged for the ticket counters, bouncing about impatiently as we inched along in one of the two endless lines. And then I spotted her, in the next line, the famous monster girl with no face. I had seen her maybe two or three other times, and it was always a shock. She was a monster girl whose face had no features. It was like looking at a blur of a face. You got the impression of holes here and there for what could have been perhaps nostrils and a mouth maybe, and eyes, like unaligned marbles amid folds and flaps of flesh and hair that looked like fur and feathers. There were rumors that the girl had been born that way, or that her face had burned off in a fire, or been cut to ribbons in a terrible car wreck or by an escaped convict crazy man with a knife. Her blur of a face was at an angle to me, and I stared at it. I couldn't help it. I blinked my eyes trying to somehow adjust them, to get them into focus, to compose something recognizable as the regular human face of a girl amid that pulpy mess of skin. Suddenly the monster girl turned her head in my direction and I jerked my eyes away. But she knew I had been staring. I could feel she knew I had been staring, and my neck burned with shame and embarrassment for her exotic horribleness. I couldn't think of anything worse than being her, a person whose face could never show her sadness, or happiness, if she ever had any, whose only expression would be *horribleness*. How could a girl with no face ever leave a dark room? How could a monster girl ever crawl out from under her rock?

Let's head for the deep end, Soldierboy, Captain said to me the minute we laid out our towels on a grassy slope above the pool that Saturday. Let's go kick that deep end's ass, Captain added, laughing that bold confident winner-of-the-Second-World-War laugh of his, and he gave my shoulder a poke with his finger that about knocked me down. I was this boney kid who had at best a baffled sense of balance. Then Captain gave me a snappy salute, which meant that I, his little soldierboy, was supposed to snap him a salute back, a little private father-son camaraderie he had initiated when I was maybe one. I knew what this meant in a heartbeat. This meant that my cowardly ass was grass and the Second World War was the mower. I hated the Second World War. This also meant Mom had ratted me out to Captain about the deep end and my cowardliness and I resolved at that moment to keep my heart hidden from everybody forever.

At noon each day when I came home from playing or school for lunch, there would be two pans heating on the stove. One pan contained simmering Campbell's tomato soup. I loved Campbell's tomato soup. A syringe and needle were being sterilized in the other bubbling water. After I had enjoyed my Campbell's tomato soup, which I slurped with infinitely slow appreciation while nibbling with elegant slowness upon the crumbs of Saltines, Mom would lead me upstairs, and I would trudge forlornly behind her like the proverbial prisoner going to the gallows. I would lie face down on my bed with my butt bared, until such time as I had worked up enough courage to gasp into my pillow a feathered, fluttering little birdy whimper of that word: *now*. Whereupon Mom would deliver into my shivery little boy butt via that needle the approximate size of a harpoon my daily dose of raging male hormones (I had had a little undescended testicle problem that took four visits to the famous Mayo Clinic to eventually make all better). While I was working up the courage to say *now*, Mom would let me jabber my head off, as I stalled. If I sensed Mom growing impatient with me, I would attempt to distract her with entertaining albeit inscrutable stories. Sometimes I would be forced to pretend to confide in Mom, telling her what I hoped would pass as truthful, private things, making my revelations as puzzling and painful as possible to engage her interest and sympathies. Hence I had told her more truthfully than I meant to about my fear of the deep end, and then I had told her about the nightmares I had had for years that as I was swimming along happily, some horrible scary creature who lived on the bottom of the deep end would awake and see me up above on the surface of the water. Whereupon in my nightmares I would feel something grab my feet from below, and pull me screaming down under the water to be eaten raw.

So there was Captain treading water in the shivery blue green water of the deep end, throwing salutes my way and hollering above the pool racket to jump on in, soldierboy, the water's right. But soldierboy just stood there looking down his at toes, curled like scared worms over the pool's edge. You can swim like a fish, soldierboy, just jump on in and swim to your old dad. I'm right here, son, nothing will happen. You won't drown, hollered Captain. But soldierboy knew he wouldn't drown. That wasn't it. Soldierboy stood there trembling. Like a cowardly leaf. Soldierboy wanted more than anything to be under the water of his beloved shallow end, holding his breath in the currents of uncomplexity at its bottom where nobody could see him. Come on now, soldierboy, Captain implored, gritting his teeth. I stared at my worried worms. Come on now, Goddamnit, Chuck, jump! Captain encouraged me and slapped the water with a cupped hand. It sounded like a shot. I flinched violently. Why don't you go ahead and jump, chickenshit, a neighborhood boy said from behind me and hooted with laughter. They were all around me, the neighborhood boys and girls, all those creepy kids with their giggles, their laughter. I spun around and ran. I pushed my way relentlessly through hooting human beings who knew me.

I skulked around that lake of a pool and slipped into the shameful shallow end on the far side, among the comforting presence of strangers, where I felt at home. I bobbed about in the shallow water, a floating head, keeping a wary eye out for Captain or any of the evil neighborhood kids, while I plotted my revenge. If only I could transform this once sweet Persian dream of a pool into a lake of acid. Or have schools of gigantic piranha churn the waves into a foam of blood. If only the creature of the deep end awoke while Captain was swimming out there all alone, when suddenly it happened, and with but a shudder of his great muscles Captain would be pulled down into the deep end, and although my old man wrestled heroically with the groping tentacles, for he was such a big brave shit, they slowly entangled him, pulling him into the dark water toward the deep end monster's huge yellow crazy eyes, and great bloody maw.

Then I heard an announcement over the clubhouse's loudspeakers. They announced that we were all honored to have Dagmar, the famous star of screen and television, as a special guest that day at Dreamland. I stood up in the shallow end and looked around wildly. *Dagmar, man oh man!* I saw a crowd passing slowly along the side of the pool by the clubhouse stairs toward the picnic area on the same slope where we had our stuff laid out. In a momentary parting of the excited throng, I was certain I caught a glimpse of utter blondeness. For a moment I considered returning to my site of shame, swallowing my pride in order to see that famous blonde person and her wondrous breasts up close. But I didn't. I had my pride. I turned and dog-paddled with dignity out to the float in the shallow end, where I pulled myself up and sat with my back to Dad and Dagmar and all they meant.

At some point, I began jumping over and over again into the pool. Time and again, I would run and hurl myself belly first from the float painfully into the choppy water. Then I would drag myself back up on the float and do it again. I didn't care. I didn't care if I knocked myself out and drowned shamefully at the bottom of the shallow end. I pictured Captain standing over where they had drug my piti-ful drowned body onto the side of the pool, blue green water draining from my mouth and nose and ears and eyes. I tried to picture Captain crying his heart out, but I couldn't. The only thing I could make come alive in my imagination was Captain carrying my limp dripping body up the clubhouse stairs while some sad song like "Endless Sea" blasted on the loud speakers, and all the evil neighborhood kids were standing around wondering out loud if I would come back from the dead and fuck with them, which, buddy, you can bet I would.

Then I pictured Dagmar swimming toward me underwater. Like a wondrous waterplant's blooming, her beautiful blonde hair floated about her head as her face came toward my own until it filled my vision. Whereupon, in the moment before I lost consciousness, I felt Dagmar's soft white arms enfold me. I was only ten years old, but I imagined myself being deliciously smothered in the immensity of Dagmar's blonde breasts as she delivered the drowning soldierboy safely to the surface.

So there I stood on the shallow end float trying to catch my breath after a particularly painful bellybuster, when a kid came directly up to me out of the basic blue and excitedly said these exact words: "Dagmar saw you, boy!" *Dagmar saw you, boy!* That kid said exactly that. I swear it! I spun around like an insane top. I looked everywhere. I looked in the water around the float. I scanned the far sides of the pool, and the grassy slopes. *Dagmar saw you, boy.* When I looked back for the kid he was gone. But that boy had been real, and he had said those exact words full of more wonder than any other words of my childhood. I swear it.

Dagmar had spotted me. That much was clear. I believed that with all of my heart. I believe it to this day. Somehow my fierce painful brave bellybusters had caught Dagmar's attention. Perhaps her blue famous eyes were settled upon me at that moment. They could be. They were. I sprang into action. I threw myself from the float like a virgin into a volcano. I exploded into that violence of water and began to swim frantically for the float in the deep end. I thrashed my arms and kicked my feet wildly. I chopped across the rough surface of the deep end, choking, my eyes burning, toward the distant float. The deep end's water strangled into my throat with each ragged stroke and it dawned on me I might never make it. It dawned on me that I might actually drown like a rat. And for what?

Fame? Fame wasn't worth it I realized. Fame wasn't worth drowning like a rat.

But at that epiphanal moment I felt strangely calm. I closed my eyes, and simply kept chopping, blindly, but unafraid, trancelike, and then suddenly I touched concrete. I slapped an astonished hand onto the surface of the float in the deep end and held on for dear life. I had not drowned like a rat after all. I had a second chance at everything, including fame. I was coughing and spitting and my sore arms trembled nearly out of control. I wiped water off of my face with my free hand and pushed my hair out of my eyes. I was there. Soldierboy had made it. Soldierboy was at the float in the deep end where he had always really belonged. Soldierboy loved that float. He gripped the edge of the float and looked around to see who had witnessed this amazing feat. He looked for the evil neighborhood kids. He looked for Dad. Soldierboy looked around for Dagmar.

And then suddenly somebody emerged from the water right beside me and grabbed the edge of the float. It was the famous girl with no face. I took one look at her and screamed. I screamed and screamed and fell back into the water, flapping my arms like crazy wings.

Happy Pills

Mark Jude Poirier

YOU AND ROBBY SIT IN ROBBY'S MESSY DORM ROOM AND WASH down the last of your wisdom-teeth codeine with Rolling Rock, while you watch a video from the sixties made for retarded girls about to hit puberty. You should be studying because it's the week before finals, but Robby's brother, who's up at Johns Hopkins, discovered a cache of old sex-ed films in a closet somewhere in the public health library, and called Robby last night. Robby took a train to Baltimore this morning to get the film, missed his organic chemistry study session, and you transferred the film to video this afternoon. You and Robby spent hours in the audio-visual lab, trying to figure out the equipment, pissing off a group of overdriven MBA students who were videotaping a presentation about conflict resolution.

The sex ed for retards film is better than you hoped. It's about menstruation, and the star is a Down's Syndrome girl named Jill who asks everyone about periods. "Does Aunt Mary get a period? Does Daddy get a period?" The climax of the film is when Jill follows her older sister into the bathroom for a maxi-pad change. Jill's sister pulls a bloody one out of her panties and straps on a fresh one with the little elastic belts they used back then. Her bush is clearly visible. You're incredulous. It's unruly. You and Robby rewind it twice and you're sure you can see pink, what Robby calls her "roast beef curtain." You can't understand why they felt the need to show this. Jill helps her sister by wrapping the bloody maxi-pad in toilet paper and carefully placing it in the trash. There's the menstrual blood. It's bright, like cherry pie filling.

You imitate Jill's voice, even though you know it's cruel and that you shouldn't. The codeine and beer make it easier. For the next few months, you use "Jill" as an adjective. Robby loses his keys and he's Jill. Your phone gets cut off because you forget to pay your bill for two months, and you are totally Jill. You keep track, though, and each time you use "Jill" as an adjective, you have to walk the five flights of stairs in your dorm. It's like a bank. You can walk the stairs before you use "Jill" as an adjective or after, but you can't owe any stairs before something important, like your econ final or your father's medical tests. If you do, you will bomb the test and your father will have cancer.

Robby is rarely Jill because he's a genius. He will go on to place second in the 1990 College Jeopardy Tournament, losing to a horse-toothed chick from Rutgers because he won't know some trivial bull-shit about the Beatles' manager. He'll win a washer and dryer and five thousand. He'll tell you that Alex Trebek wears thick makeup.

Two months after that, his sister will find him on the floor of the laundry room of their parents' sprawling Nantucket house. He will be clutching a tin of shoe polish. His headphones will still be blaring De La Soul, he'll be wearing your old lacrosse shorts, and he will have a bluish pallor. He will be dead.

The grief will take residence in your stomach and make it difficult for you to return to D.C. for your senior year. Your parents will say it's okay if you want to take a semester off, think about things, see a few professionals. But you'll return that fall, and when you realize no one on campus has even a vague sense of humor, no one is good at wasting time like Robby was, you'll actually study and do well and graduate on time and stop using "Jill" as an adjective.

You take Paxil. Twenty milligrams per day. One pink oval pill before you go to bed. On the television commercials for Paxil, a woman can't cope at work. A man is afraid to meet people at a party. They touch their foreheads to show inner turmoil. All the actors in the commercials are attractive, with smooth skin and nicely combed hair. Even though you feel the commercials are comically unrealistic, you know these pills have helped. You no longer have an anxious pang in your gut, you no longer suffer bouts of super can't-get-out-of-bed depression, and you no longer count your steps or have to enter a room with your right foot and leave with your left. The nocturnal teeth grinding has ceased, and your jaw has stopped clicking. You can eat bagels again.

You could be a spokesperson for Paxil except that you're a district marketing manager for Lilly, the company that produces Prozac. You tried to like Prozac, you tried really hard, but you couldn't sleep, and after about a month, you started to look like your alcoholic grandfather, full purple bags under your bloodshot eyes. It was better than Desiprimine, though, the drug they put you on after college, which made you a constipated zombie and left you a legacy of hemorrhoids that flare up when you eat Mexican food or have mustard on a sandwich.

You keep your pills in your suit pocket because the airlines have lost your bags twice this year. Lost for good. A mad scramble for receipts, and several arguments with airline employees trained to detect when someone is lying. Your Paxil was in there, and you spent that first out-of-town meeting dizzy and nauseated from withdrawal until you had time to find a twenty-four-hour pharmacy. When you finally took the pill, about a day and a half late, you felt as if you could feel the happiness chemicals burrowing into the crinkles of your brain.

You sit in coach, and the woman seated next you, a big potato with dull brown hair, is chattering on about where you should eat in Indianapolis. You already told her that you've been to Indianapolis before, you are familiar with its restaurants, but she won't shut up about a sports bar that she thinks you would love. "They have one room for football, one for basketball, and . . ."

But you are thinking about Amy. She's your wife. Married four years, and you're pretty sure that you hate her. The elaborate scene unfolds: Amy in an elevator, heading up to an abortion clinic in the sky, the one hundred and thirty-seventh floor, the cables snap, and she begins to fall, the bell chiming for each floor she passes, she rises like an astronaut, she is pinned against the ceiling, the bell chimes, faster and faster—*ding ding ding ding ding*—but Amy has plenty of time to know that she's about to die. She has time to regret. She has time to think that she's selfish and cruel. One of her shoes has come off. It floats below her. She wants it. She wants her shoe, a pointy Gucci sling-back, something a witch might wear to a barbecue, and she fights the G-force to reach for it, barely touching the stick heel with the tip of her fingernail before the crash. You take comfort in knowing that this animosity toward your wife and these vivid scenes can be controlled, perhaps with a simple increase in your Paxil dosage. From 20 mg to 40 mg.

You pull the *Sky Mall* catalog from the seat pocket. You flip to a page called 'Successories'. Your ironic favorite item is a poster of a husky dog with the quotation: THE ATTITUDE OF THE LEADER DETERMINES THE SPEED OF THE PACK. You wonder how your sales team would respond if you spouted something like that at your next meeting. You turn to the monotonous hag next to you who is still speaking and you say, "Quiet time."

"Excuse me?" she mumbles. You notice her neck skin is loose— like she lost a significant amount of weight. Hundreds of pounds. Good for her.

"It's quiet time," you say. "Please abide by the rules."

You can't play kickball because they have already chosen teams and they're in the fourth inning. Chris Zizza says you can, but Doug says no way. You wish you had done your math last night like you were supposed to and that Mrs. Campobello didn't make you stay in at lunch until it was done, until now. You want to play second base and hang out with your teammates. There is safety in numbers. Thelma never comes over to the kickball game. You saw her this morning, so you know she's here, somewhere, maybe over near the swings with her friends, or outside the science room playing Chinese jump rope and grunting like she does.

You have every reason to be afraid of Thelma. She is retarded and smells like your grandmother, like cigarette smoke and cleaning fluid. Her eyes are crazy; there is nothing behind them. She is a Metco kid, bussed in from Boston. She has freckles even though she is black. If she decides to get you, she will, and everyone will help her. Everyone will chase you. When they catch you, they will hold you down while she kisses you and licks you and squeezes your balls. Teachers never stop her.

Thelma caught you once in the beginning of the year. Patches of melted early-fall snow dotted the playground. Your back and hair were muddy when they finally let you up. You were crying and you couldn't breathe. Thelma's tongue felt bigger than it looked. She wasn't seeing you. She was only seeing your mouth.

The Thelma attack returns with an unwelcome carnal immediacy that scares you into action. You jog off into the woods, back behind the janitor's building, where you and your friends once found a dead cat—back when you had friends, before everyone didn't think you were weird, before Margaret Hickey told everyone on the bus you had a boner when you really didn't, which was a miracle because you often did get boners on the bouncy bus, especially in the morning. You wait for the bell to ring. You pee against a tree and are amazed to see steam rising from your piss. It doesn't seem that cold out. You turn over a log and look for salamanders, but this log has been turned over many times before by many science classes, and nothing alive is under it.

Later in the year, four older boys will bring Thelma to this very spot in the woods. Rumors will fly. Thelma sucked all of their dicks. They poked her pussy with a stick. They fucked her. Rumors will escalate to such an extent that the principal will call an assembly where he tells the whole fourth, fifth, and sixth grade what really happened: Thelma brought some marijuana from Boston for the boys to try. Nothing sexual happened. Because you live in a community of rich, concerned parents, a few moms will take time off from shopping and planning meals to come to school and talk to each of the classes individually about drugs and sex. They will be trained by an educational psychologist for one afternoon before doing so. Doug's mom is pretty, you will think—like the lady on the shampoo bottle: fluffy blonde hair and big eyes. She will field questions, along with your teacher, Mrs. Campobello, about marijuana and rumors you will have heard about Thelma. Kim Pond will ask what marijuana is. The word "marijuana" scares you and it will scare you then. You will be surprised that kids at your school smoke it or would want to. You will wonder if they are likely to go crazy and stab you with knives. As if Leonard Nimoy and killer bees and UFOs weren't enough to worry about. You have heard a few things about Charles Manson and Helter Skelter. You are not allowed to watch the movie on TV. Your cousin Stephen has a *Helter Skelter* book, a thick floppy paperback, and in the middle there is a section of photographs. You looked at them once, saw Manson's crazy eyes, the hippie girls who followed him, the victims, the messy crime scenes. You will never look at those photographs again, and when Stephen wants to play Helter Skelter, you

will say you have a stomach ache. But you will fear—you'll be sure—
that if you don't play Helter Skelter with Stephen, some day you will
be murdered by drug-crazed psychos. After going inside, presumably
to lie down, the fear consumes you, and you will change your mind
and run outside and find Stephen and tell him yes, yes you will play
Helter Skelter, of course. The game won't be that scary. Stephen will
yell, "There they are!" and you will both run the other way until he
yells it again, and you turn around and run again. Over and over. For
an hour or so. You will think he should call the game "There They
Are" instead of "Helter Skelter."

Your hotel in Indianapolis is a square. It looks like it should be
part of an office park on a road with a name like "Service Lane West"
or "Passway 102." It edges a sad public university, a branch of Indiana
State, or Purdue, or Indiana University. All the buildings on campus
look like shipping and receiving centers. Peering out your window
tonight, you see no students. The grass is brown and patchy under
yellow lights. You are thankful that you went to a nice university with
attractive buildings that weren't built in this century. It's March 30,
and when you landed in Indianapolis three hours late at 5:03 P.M., the
pilot told you it was eighteen degrees outside. The woman next to
you broke the Quiet Time rule and hesitantly said, "A little colder
than Los Angeles, huh?" Now you place your suitcase on the bed and
question your decision to come to Indianapolis a few days early. It's
better than being at home with Amy, though, you promise yourself
that.

Amy won't look you in the eye when she tells you. You wonder if
she would have even told you if you hadn't asked. You would have
eventually asked, noticed that she wasn't getting bigger, noticed when
September rolled around that you didn't have a baby son or daughter. "There was either something wrong with the fetus, or something
wrong with me," she tells the table. She doesn't use the word "baby"
and you ask her why. "Fourteen weeks does not a baby make." She
seems more annoyed than sad. You want to puke. You want to smack
Amy. You want to leave. In minutes, you will decide to go to
Indianapolis a few days early. You wonder if it's the Paxil that scram-
bled the genetic code in your sperm, made your baby a retard with its

heart on the outside of its body. You know Amy is lying, that she aborted your baby. It's a bit too convenient to have a miscarriage a week after the tests, which, she said, went well, and showed the baby to be in good health. Wrong. It showed something else, the worst, and she couldn't handle it. "I would appreciate it," she says as she walks out of the kitchen, "if you tell the truth and say I miscarried to anyone who cares, and keep your creepy paranoia to yourself." You want to pick up the butter dish in front of you and hurl it at Amy. It would be nice to nail her in the back of the head, to get butter in her hair. You don't even bother yelling at her. You long for the Midwest. Polite, wholesome people. Tough people. Hard workers. People who aren't tan. You decide now that a few extra days in Indianapolis might do you some good. "I'm fine!" Amy yells from upstairs. "I'm fucking fine! Thanks for asking! Thanks for your fucking concern!"

You don't remember downtown Indianapolis being all part of a giant mall. Skywalks stretch and snake from office buildings, to hotels, to restaurants, to department stores. A giant Habitrail. There's a food court around every corner of every skywalk. It's freezing outside, so you don't mind that downtown is now a giant tangled mess of careless architecture, though you are aware that this sort of over-the-top retail has stripped Indianapolis of any individuality it may have once possessed. You recall it having individuality, but you can't be sure.

You walk into Sam Goody Music and you're greeted by a robotic voice: *Welcome to Sam Goody*. The source of the welcome is a deformed woman awkwardly perched in a wheelchair. When a customer walks in, she presses a button on a panel that sits in her lap: *Welcome to Sam Goody*. You don't look closely at her. You can't. Is it nice that Sam Goody has given her this job, the job of greeter? They could be using her. People will assume that Sam Goody is charitable company for employing the handicapped and the same people won't think twice about spending $18.99 on a CD that they could get at Target for $11.99. You begin to flip through the common overpriced CDs, and, like every time you're in a CD store, your bowels tell you to find a toilet fast.

You push through throngs of tanned kids just back from spring break. They wear faux retro T-shirts that advertise gas stations, pizza parlors, and sport teams that never existed. Where are their winter coats? As you walk through a food court on the way to the rest rooms, you notice that people in Indianapolis eat poorly—fried chicken, Cinnabons, barbecued ribs—and are generally overweight. You decide that you too will eat poorly this week, beginning with a cheeseburger after you finish in the bathroom.

The stall you have chosen is the cleanest you have ever been in. Leave it to good midwesterners to make their public rest rooms pleasant. The person who cleaned it most likely did so with a genuine smile and a firm sense of pride. There is no graffiti. The tile work is actually interesting, sort of southwestern influenced, navy and terra cotta. It doesn't stink. You know you won't catch anything from this toilet, so you sit right down and think you could stay here forever.

As you enjoy your cheeseburger and fries and onion rings and deep-fried mozzarella sticks in one of the food courts, you realize that you can find a deformed or mentally retarded person no matter where you look. You will always be able to do so. You look around until you spot a man with only one leg wheeling into Abercrombie & Fitch.

Amy is out. You don't know where and you don't care. It is only seven months into your marriage, you're sitting on a leather couch that cost more than your last car, trying to relax in your new house in Rancho Palos Verdes that set you back seven hundred thousand because of its ocean view and good school district, and you don't care where your wife is. It would be very easy for you to get in your car and drive three miles to the video store and pick out a porno, but the Paxil makes masturbation an arduous and often exasperating experience, so you opt to flip through the channels and eat an avocado sandwich.

You stop on a documentary about Down's Syndrome kids whose parents want them to have plastic surgery to make them look as if they aren't retarded. The idea repulses you. You decide the parents are doing it for themselves, not for their kids. You then wonder if Down's Syndrome kids have a camaraderie. They do all look alike. You saw some in South America who looked like twins of ones you've seen in the U.S., only with darker skin. Jill with darker skin. If one sees another in the supermarket is there some sort of atavistic recognition and sympathetic attachment between them? You think, yes, and that these vile parents are robbing their kids of one the few special feelings they might have during their short lives. You are disgusted by the doctors who perform these surgeries, grossed out that someone even thought of doing it in the first place. You finish your sandwich and head to the video store.

When you return, you see Amy's car in the driveway, so you turn around and take back the porno unwatched.

You slept really well last night. Ten solid hours. While the ugly patterned bedspread was made of an abrasive synthetic material, the mattress was perfect: soft with a hard center. The sleep makes coming early to Indianapolis worth it.

Other people from Lilly have begun to inhabit the hotel. You see them in the lobby and in the halls, men and women from all over the world, shades of skin ranging from deep black to nearly translucent. Some wear turbans. Others are in ill-fitted suits from the Third World. Bad eyewear from Eastern Europe. Good eyewear from Western Europe. Dots on foreheads. Accents. Almost everyone carries a black leather Lilly folder. Most smile. You smile. You don't even want coffee this morning. You look forward to spending the day in the mall, perhaps catching a movie, eating poorly again.

You share a cab with Oswaldo, an Ecuadorian with *90210* sideburns. He wears a well-tailored suit. He's in charge of launching the Prozac Weekly campaign in three South American countries.

"Ah, eh, Indy is pleasing to you, no?" he asks as you drive out of the hotel's parking lot. His breath is visible.

The cold vinyl seat has drained all warmth from your ass. "I like it well enough," you say. "Too cold."

"I like it very much," he says, grinning, looking through the cab's window at the brown, freezing gloom.

You have been to Ecuador. You and Robby were there for three weeks between sophomore and junior years. You smoked a lot of pot. You got food poisoning and puked for two days in a hostel called the Magic Bean. A nice girl from Australia helped you, made you sip bottled water and take showers. You lost almost ten pounds in forty-eight hours. When you finally stopped puking, Robby brought you Gatorade and convinced you to get on a bus with him to a jungle town called

Mindo. As hard as you try, you cannot remember much of the few days you spent in Mindo because you ate some psychedelic mushrooms. You visited a reptile zoo, you know that. You have a snapshot of you and Robby holding a giant boa—although, that may have been back in Quito. You remember crawling under a building in Mindo, finding a shoe in the mud, and hundreds of tiny black and orange frogs, the size of crickets, jumping all over you. Nothing else.

"Where are you from?" the cab driver suddenly asks.

You can't tell if he's asking you or Oswaldo, so you answer for the both of you. "I'm from Los Angeles and Oswaldo is from Quito, Ecuador."

"You a Jew?" he asks you.

"What?"

"A Jew from California?"

"I am a Jew," you lie, wondering what he's getting at.

"You look like a Jew," he mumbles. "A Jew and a Mexican in my cab at the same time." He breathes audibly through his nose.

"Oswaldo is from Ecuador, not Mexico," you say. "You have a problem with us?" The cab driver is scaring you. His hair is thin and greasy. His face is pink. The back of his neck is cratered with acne scars.

"I have lots of problems!" he yells. You notice the letters DARE tattooed across his red knuckles. The letters have faded into a dirty green color.

"What is happen?" Oswaldo asks you.

"El es un racista," you tell Oswaldo, wondering if "racista" is even a Spanish word.

Oswaldo nods.

"Let us off at the gas station up there," you tell the driver through a nervous lump in your throat.

But he doesn't stop. Instead, he takes a right on a road, which you're pretty sure isn't leading to downtown. "Come on!" you yell. "Let us out!" You would just jump out of the cab at the next light if it weren't for Oswaldo. You can't leave him alone. You can't tell him to jump out. You can't remember the word for "jump" in Spanish.

"Where are we going to?" Oswaldo asks.

"I don't know," you say. "He is loco."

Oswaldo laughs nervously.

The driver mumbles something about all Mexicans being sodomite faggots.

Your cell phone is charging at the hotel, sitting on the bathroom counter. You're Jill for not taking it with you.

Is this it? Is this Nazi redneck it?

"Stop this cab!" you yell. You try to open the window, but it's locked. You pound on it. "This is ridiculous!" Warehouses and run-down, winter-beaten homes. Dirt lots. A spray-painted, gutted-out bus. A few crows pecking at a shredded mattress in someone's front yard. The buildings thin out. Not even a neighborhood. The sky is brown. The cab speeds ahead. Oswaldo prays aloud.

Think of strangling the driver from behind, or at least pulling his greasy hair. Imagine the cab crashing into one of the formidable trees that line the road. There are no seatbelts.

You could be honest with the driver, tell him you're thirty-three, you're not Jewish, you're married but don't like your wife who you think recently aborted your unborn child without consulting you because she found out it was defective, you take Paxil but work for Lilly, the company that keeps Indianapolis alive, although you wonder why they don't move their world headquarters to a decent city. You could go on. You could tell him about the time you saw your grandmother in the hall in the middle of the night, a rubber tube hanging from her asshole like a tail. Tell him about the long-haired kid outside a T station in Boston, blasting White Snake on a boom box, playing air-guitar with a fucked-up arm. And speaking of fucked-up arms: that beggar kid in the bus station in Quito. His arm was more like a foot, his fingers all like baby toes. Ask the driver if he thinks the kid's mom worked in some horrible chemical factory when she was pregnant. That same day, a guy carried a woman onto the bus, sat her down across the aisle from you and Robby. Her feet were on backwards, no shit. If she had looked down, she would have seen her heels, not her toes. Even Robby couldn't come up with anything funny to say. You were both depressed until you reached your destination a few hours later. Can this driver think of anything to say about that? Did you hear the one about the lady with the backwards feet?

The driver stops the cab. "Get out," he says. "Get out of my cab." He unlocks the doors and you step onto the frozen dirt. He drives away, leaving you and Oswaldo among naked trees.

"I am confuse," Oswaldo says. "It is cold."

Oswaldo is handsome. A wonderful mixture of European and native Ecuadorian features, so perfect you want to cry. You know it's all just a rush of chemicals in your brain that's making you feel this way, a wave of relief that washes the right receptors and lights them up like Christmas trees with a perfect cocktail of neurotransmitters, but it's real nonetheless, and you're part of it and it's part of you. Oswaldo smiles and looks around. You hug him; you have to. You bury your nose in his sideburn, breathe in his cologne and the cold air, hug him tighter. He hugs you back, and you feel like everything bad falls away.

Models and Monsters

Jason Fox

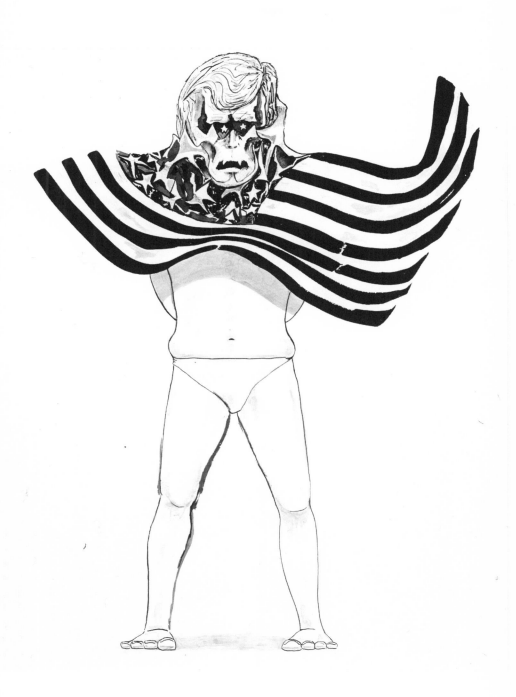

My Mother and the Stranger

Saïd Sayrafiezadeh

MY MOTHER'S NAME IS MARTHA HARRIS, WHILE MY NAME, ON the other hand, as you already know from the byline, is Saïd Sayrafiezadeh. If we lived in a matriarchal society, my last name would also be Harris. I would be a Harris right now sitting down to write this story this evening about the evening a stranger forced his way into my mother's home, if men did not—do not—view women as property. This going back thousands of years, a history I am unfamiliar with, have not researched with any authority, yet know it to be somehow true as I sit down to write, decidedly not a Harris.

It is twenty-nine years ago when this tale takes place. It is 1973. It is Fort Greene, Brooklyn. It is nighttime. I am five years old. My mother is forty. She gave birth to me when she was thirty-five, and by thirty-six she was separated from my father.

Shortly after the abrupt and unceremonious departure of my father, who also happened to be her husband of ten years, my mother abandoned the name Sayrafiezadeh and returned to her maiden name of Harris. "He gave me twenty-four hours notice," my mother has told me dramatically more than once. And I imagine the scene unfolding in the perfunctory way it does when one is laid off, effective immediately, and escorted from the building. My mother's return to Harris was a way to be away from Sayrafiezadeh, it was a way to divorce herself from my father who would not legally divorce himself from my mother for twenty more years, that is until he was ready to remarry again, and his legal status in the United States was no longer in jeop-

59

ardy. But my mother's return to Harris not only succeeded in divorcing herself from her ex-husband but also of divorcing herself from her present-son. Written on the mailbox in the lobby of our apartment building was "Harris/Sayrafiezadeh," as if roommates resided there, or an unmarried couple, or a progressive married couple, a progressive married interracial couple at that.

"Supper is almost ready," my mother calls to me twenty-nine years ago when this story begins. Together we are alone in our apartment. I am playing on the floor in the living room, while my mother is busying herself in the kitchen. I place this colored wooden block on top of that colored wooden block. Silence surrounds me, interrupted only by the faint clink-clank of my mother's dishes in the sink. It is that time of night in New York City when everything seems to fall silent and still. And on the sixteenth floor of the apartment building we live in, everything is even more silent and more still, the sounds from the street falling short of us. And it is also at this time of night, for reasons unbeknownst to the scientists, that strangers choose to enter people's homes unannounced and do evil things. It is during this pre-supper séance then that the stranger, who has decided against being detected in the elevator and has climbed sixteen flights, enters our apartment and silently, stealthily, creeps, quietly, whisperly behind my mother and waits. His presence my mother and I are unaware of.

I have lied to you, reader. My mother's name is not Martha Harris. I have lied and I apologize for it. My mother's name is, in fact, Martha Finklestein. I am sketchy on the details, because my mother is sketchy on the details, but sometime during World War II when my mother was about ten years old and living in Mount Vernon, New York, her father decided that his eldest son would have an easier go at finding a job if he was not so obviously Jewish. Thus in one swift pen stroke the family did away with Finklestein forever, replacing it with the generic and rather boring Harris that I first introduced my mother to you as. If we lived in a matriarchal society and if we lived in a society that did not have its own history of anti-Semitism, I would be writing this story tonight not as a Harris, but as a Finklestein. But since none of this is the case, I use the byline Sayrafiezadeh. The Jew in me has been completely supplanted by the Iranian.

My mother is in the kitchen. She has called out to me that supper is almost ready. And now she turns from the dishes, innocently, turns with whatever collection of inconsequential thoughts are running through her mind at that moment, and turns to see not the empty space she had imagined and wholeheartedly expected, but to see the space filled with the large form of the dastardly stranger, who has been waiting patiently, because he has known that she will see him eventually, turn toward him eventually, the way a spider knows that the fly will eventually have no choice but to fly into its web. And my mother screams. It breaks irreparably the silence of the evening as well as the world of my colored wooden blocks. And the dish my mother is holding in her hand drops and shatters on the floor, giving a nice exclamation to the drama at hand.

My mother is a Jewish woman, I've already said. You can tell this by the name she does not go by. You can also tell, I have always thought, by her physical features. Her prominent nose, for instance. Her tiny, five-foot-one frame, the hunched way she has about her, the old beyond-her-years attitude. She was a senior citizen by the time this story takes place, at age forty. Of course, none of these features may have anything to do with Jewishness, but rather with my own anti-Semitic associations, which I admit I am in great possession of. In ways that I am not quite clear about, but will defend as if they can be proven mathematically, I have always asserted that my mother's Jewishness is why I have found her so ugly my entire life, and why as her offspring I have often found myself to be so ugly. It is certainly not helped by the fact that my mother does not have her hair done, does not wear makeup, does not paint her nails, does not wear perfume, does not dress in colorful, fitted outfits, does not date men ever, does not have sex with men ever, does not exhibit any sexuality, homosexual, asexual, or otherwise. The last man she had sex with was my father, which was when she was thirty-six years old. My mother, in effect, took a vow of celibacy after my father's departure, and became a nun, a secular nun, a secular Jewish nun. When my mother walks down the street in what amounts to her habit, men are not compelled to look at her tits or ass. And the one time she wore a skirt I was confused and made vaguely uncomfortable by the sight of her calves and thighs in stockings, uncomfortable in the way one is when one watches a handicapped person attempting to dance, for instance. It is a painful attempt. All of these details I have somehow come to associate with the fact that she is Jewish, and I am happy to have that part of myself disguised, suppressed, repressed, hiding the mother in me away, happy to not be a Finklestein, happy to have been born into a patriarchal society.

And my mother turns, sees, screams, and the plate breaks, and my child's play on the floor with colored blocks promptly comes to an end. I rise fearfully, and pad toward the kitchen, peeking cautiously around the corner, imagining the worst, imagining myself saving my mother and in turn being saved by her.

In the kitchen my mother stands erect, paralyzed, her back presses against the refrigerator, the stranger faces her menacingly from across the counter where he leans. His size is overwhelming, and made doubly so by the fact that there have been no adult men in our apartment since my father's exit. The stranger is bulbous, and he casts a shadow that falls across the kitchen, across my mother and myself. We are infected by his shadow. My mother is motionless like a cadaver, rigid with fear. The stranger is motionless, too, but his posture is loose, relaxed, an athlete about to take off. Better to be relaxed when you are the assailant. My mother and the stranger watch each other, they wait, they plot, each wondering what the other's first move will be.

A brief word about the missing patriarch. My father has gone off to work diligently attempting to overthrow this society of ours. He is a subversive. He is a communist. He is a Trostkyite. He has lived in exile. He has also spent time in jail. He writes long articles with phrases lifted directly from Marx and the Russian Revolution. Articles that the coal mining layman would have difficulty deciphering. He refers to his fellow party members as "comrades." In my mother's home there is a reverence for my father, he is a divinity and I am taught by my mother to be happy and proud and respectful of the work he is doing to better the world. This is all I am going to say about my father. He is a figure in the world, but a non-figure in our lives. Nor is he what I have sat down to write about tonight.

Tonight I am writing about how a stranger has managed to ingeniously infiltrate a double-locked door. And my mother speaks to me in a low, breathy whisper, as if knowing she will be granted one wish and one wish only. "Get me," she says, "go get me a shoe." And I do as I am told. I scamper into the closet for her weapon of choice, and return to her at once, where she clutches the shoe in her hand.

Said Sayrafiezadeh

The stranger sees this weapon and does not like it. The balance of power has shifted, he knows this. There has been an unexpected sea change. He was attracted by the smells of dinner and he thought that his jaunt through the kitchen would be an easy one, that he would collect his three or four crumbs into his basket and be gone before anyone so much as noticed. He has done this many times before, this is how he has survived and made his living.

"You son of a bitch," my mother is saying and the tone of her voice frightens me and frightens the stranger, and his antennae begin to move this way and that, trying to map out the best possible escape route. And he moves away from my mother abruptly, quickly, his six footsteps patting out a rhythm across the counter, over a plate, and up the side of the Maxwell House Coffee can where he stops to survey the lay of the land, catch his breath, and gather his bearings.

And where we can observe him more closely. He is, to put it mildly, a behemoth. The subject of legends, of folklore. He stands nearly six inches, with antennae which add another six inches. We notice a scar running along one of his legs, from the knee down. When he looks, we can see where he is looking. We can make out the consternation on his face. A single bead of sweat breaks on his forehead and falls, plunking into the Maxwell House Coffee can.

"Where did I enter from?" He says to himself, angry at himself for having lost the way. "Where did I enter from? I was sure it was from over here!"

From where she stands, my mother raises the shoe like a gunman taking aim. The insect has no choice but to move, caught in the crosshairs. My mother raises the shoe higher. The insect moves more quickly, scurrying further along the counter, and then down into the sink, and then up the sink where he hangs upside down from the faucet.

"If I don't move, perhaps she won't see me here." The thought of a delusional man. A man whose options are slowly running out.

And now my mother, having summoned her courage, begins to move toward him.

Once very late at night, well past midnight, my mother carried me in her arms home from the Clinton-Washington subway station in Fort Greene, Brooklyn. It's the G line. She walked along a completely empty Dekalb Avenue and from nowhere a man suddenly appeared and stood in our way. I remember his face clearly. I was in my mother's arms so I was at eye level with him, an odd perspective for a child so used to looking up toward adults, and I made eye contact with him. We looked at each other briefly. My mother stepped to her left and the man stepped to his right, blocking her. My mother stepped to her right and the man stepped to his left, blocking her again.

Now my mother and I are running across the wall, knowing that if we can make it to the cabinet we will find safety. Safety among the plates and cups and bowls. He'll never find us in there, my mother whispers to me. We will be safe in there. We will hide ourselves in the maze of the dishes and we will wait and wait until he has exhausted himself from hunting for us and gives up. If it takes hours, we will wait for hours. If it takes days, we will wait for days. And when he has finally exhausted himself, bored himself and turned the light off and left the kitchen we will emerge and return home and pick up where we left off.

Reader, I have lied to you twice. I promised I would not bring my father into this description. But how could I avoid the obvious? Couldn't we, my mother and I, have used him now? A strong, large man to set the world in order. He, no doubt, would have reasoned with my mother and the cockroach. He would have shown them that their oppression is the same oppression. He would have shown how the ruling class exploits my mother in the same way it exploits the insect. "They tell you that there is only supply enough for one of you," he would explain in his emphatic accented English. "And in this way they pit the two of you against one another in order to drive down your wages and increase their profit. This is a historical fact. Marx has written extensively about it." Perhaps he would even have some literature to give out. And in this clear reasoning of my father, the bug would see this, and understand. And my mother would see this, and understand. A sweet reconciliation between them would ensue. And then my father would be off, to save and educate the other workers.

But as I have said, my father is not present. This bloody task is up to my mother and my mother alone. And the bug passes by the bowl of beans, pausing ever so briefly. "My, that would have made for a nice snack," it thinks wistfully, using that far off calm inner voice that one uses for thinking thoughts during the most inappropriate moments. And in this pause within a pause my mother finally, swiftly, brings the shoe down, catching the insect on its shell, knocking it off the counter and onto the floor where it lands on its back.

The pain ricochets through its body. It has felt pain before, but never pain like this. It knows the situation is dire. "I'm OK," it thinks in the way you think when you have dislocated your shoulder or broken your leg, and you are trying to convince and comfort yourself that you have not dislocated your shoulder or broken your leg and that all you really need is a good night's sleep and you'll be as good as new in the morning. The psychologists have discovered that in times of duress we will often lie to ourselves and evade the lie simultaneously. "Here I go, you see," the bug says to himself, "right back on my feet, you see, and right around the corner of the counter, to the oven, as I planned from the start." But as it races toward the oven, it is unaware that now it is moving at half the speed it was before. And my mother, mercilessly, strikes the bug again. The pain again. Ricocheting again. Commingling with the former pain. Suddenly feeling numb, drowsy, wouldn't it be nice to just sleep right here in the corner, curl up in the corner. Just a short pre-supper nap. But no! Now is not the time for sleep! I must continue or all is lost! But wouldn't it be nice?

And my mother again, like a matador. And again. The sport suddenly cheapened for the pleasure of the lower classes.

The cockroach is still now, quiet. Resting on its back. It's antennae involuntarily waving this way and that, still trying to pick up the good news, though there is no good news it can pick up that will do it any good. So this is how it will end, it thinks. Here on this cold linoleum floor in these fools' apartment. There's still so much I wanted to do with my life. I would have wished for a better parting. In the arms of my lover. With my children gathered around. Will they know of my death? Who will inform them? They will wait up tonight, hoping for me to return with the goodies that I promised. They will wait the next day and the next. And they will always wonder after me.

And my mother is sobbing now, great sobs shaking her body, tears and snot running down her face, the exhaustion that comes after the execution, the exhaustion of the hangman who weeps after the trapdoor has been pulled, the prolonged involvement leading to the condemned's death has left him susceptible to his most vulnerable emotions. And my mother suddenly scoops me into her arms and sits down in the kitchen chair clutching me tightly. Her fingers digging into my back. Her body heaves, waves of grief, and I go up and down in those waves. The ocean's moan in my ear. Tears for a lost family, poverty, uncertainty, tears for a distant, nonexistent husband. We sit there together, the three of us, she in the kitchen chair, I in her lap, the cockroach on the floor, fading away, it's life slowly ebbing from its pores. The moments. My mother's moments, my moments, the insect's moments, all together in one moment. The deathwatch filling the room. The bug feeling no pain now. The contradiction: in great pain, no pain. My mother rocking back and forth, clutching me, I her teddy bear. The three of us all witnessing the cascading moment that is coming, coming, comes. And then passes. The antennae still. And the cockroach gone. My mother and I alone again. We will be the only living witnesses to what transpired in that night.

It Takes a Nation of Millions to Hold Us Back

William Bowers

ON THE PORCH, EARLY EVENING: A PROWLING EGRET, A TASTE OF rain. My personal palm gestures, as if congratulating itself. The clumsy young wives have formed coalitions to combat "the cat problem." Some nights, a man can be seen sleepwalking his lawnmower. I take up too much space. Have you heard the one about a white man, a black man, and a Polack, slouching toward Bethlehem to be born?

This time last year, I was wishing there were something funny about being in the Art Institute of Chicago with a Meredith, a failing love—who'd do anything to my body to put me to sleep—counting the Jesuses hanging side-by-side around us like a rowing team in a yearbook photo. We kept segregated tallies of how many painters painted how many nails, how many had his mama reaching out, how many gave him a little stoop to stand on.

Meredith championed mass martyrdoms. She was probably ill. She was ill. She'd say, "Every now and then, a few of us need to be crushed beneath the weight of what we take to be God's hands." She'd say, "Our time is always running out." She'd say, "We need another theodontist." She'd say, "We need some new, suicidal pioneers." Now she does folk art on saw blades and acts like it matters.

I miss my old neighborhood and that's that. I used to think people who did crossword puzzles were sad. I am still amazed that nicknames have been a cultural quantity since before the Roman empire. My neighbor the pilot is probably reporting "everything's calm where we're headed." My old yard didn't boast such infuriating solvency.

And its oak, what a sight: choked by ivy riders, strip-searched by the wind.

Distant heat lightning: et cetera borealis. Correction notices for atmospheric misprints. Malfunctions in the cosmic lobby's lighting.

This happens every this-time-of-year. Around mid-October. I look at photo albums too long on consecutive nights. Old backyards become lost empires. Even nondescript uncles take on epic significance. The further I get from these little bonfires, the more I burn.

Okay, I miss Meredith. Winter, drunk, we'd sleep off Carolina's stunts, wake to Leigh and Gable bitching over banisters. I thought we'd grow old, and get to ignore our accidental offspring. When she left, the place where she'd stood seemed to freeze, barely everything.

We met at a thrift store pinned between Meticulous Motors and Patriotic Title Loans. Scavenger Country, where mothers sorted through bargain crosses, monitored by half-mannequins in mismatched clothes, the radio telling them what love is. Within minutes of our meeting, Meredith, charged with sorting out the universe's mess, was ranting about how "we are an igneous, purgative people who prefer asphalt to the ocean, that unsellable place where the power lines stop." Outside the store, the kids who owned the world breezed by in silver Hondas, the sun co-opting their perfect skin. I was just a tourist, smitten to be in a city that wasn't my fault.

She could have used her standard-issue horrible parents as an excuse to piss her life away, but she yielded. Her life's an ongoing process of almost forgiving them. My horoscope says I will live to see more snow.

Not too long ago, she sent me a sexy postcard as a joke: a brunette exiting a hotel pool in one of those old-fashioned swimsuits. One morning she waited with a broom on the porch for every single leaf.

The day I had to have her arrested, her friend Donnie Canning, that fat Hejaz freezer merchant, came to see me.

"Men, in times like these, should party naked," was what he said. We went to his boat, where he had hoped to drink himself to death. A storm destroyed his chances though, sunk it. The day it sank, he stared at the water and said, "Well, shit. How am I going to die now?"

I didn't break down until those clipboard people came to take the neighbor's baby.

"Sweet ladies, stay in your graves," I like to say to the grannies I imagine to be buried in my yard. We've run out of heresies. "Sweet ladies, whisper if you want me to keep you."

My friend who owns a Christmas tree farm says for a few dollars I could just chop.

You have to pay to park here now. Hordes go by my porch along the edges of their lives. Caligula wished his people had one neck. Two suits on the corner are wielding toothpicks viciously, perhaps telling sweaty stories, trying to forget their secretaries' monotonous lips. The suits move apart: time to go home, and take up again the burden of community. Meredith said that "municipalities are allergic to perfection." I stay unsalvageably ill-informed about current events. Life in this country, at this time, is, if you choose to let it be, ridiculously simple. Banks are electric shoeboxes. Police keep all the evil out.

I was once kissed randomly, at night, on this street. When I told Donnie Canning about it, he asked, "How do you know it wasn't a whore nostalgic for a freebie?" I'd like a mercenary pen pal. I might place an ad. She, if it's a she, will never have to meet me.

Nor will it be required that the sentiments we share be honest. Each letter should simply tell me what I want to hear, and end with love, and then a name for it to stick to.

Oh for Chrissakes. Join the human race (Wheeler, page 115)

Amends

Cynthia Weiner

THERE WERE THREE PHRASES, ALEX ONCE HEARD, THAT LOST ALL sincerity if spoken on request: *I love you, thank you*, and *I'm sorry*. She thought about this often in her first month clean. It was August, and amends was the topic at nearly every meeting she went to. Eighth month, Eighth Step—"We made a list of all persons we had harmed, and became willing to make amends to them all."

She was nowhere near the amends process; one step at a time, they said at meetings, and she hadn't even looked at the First yet. But at times she thought she might skip over the rest and dive straight into the Eighth. She liked the idea of a list. She could make lists for hours, sitting at her kitchen table with a pen and a pad of clean white paper. Shampoo & cat food. Call: Mom, dentist?, library. Exercise, brown rice, find a job. "Persons" she liked too, the civic anonymity of it, the statutory zip.

Except "willing" she wasn't so sure about, and "harmed" gave her a headache. At "harmed" she skipped to the next page of the pad and started again. Milk, aspirin, Diet Coke—bottles not cans!

"Be glad you didn't get clean last month," her friend Ritchie said. They were outside the church during the smoking break, leaning against the fence that enclosed a small patch of brown grass with a couple of tired-looking daisies.

"Every day was the Seventh Step," he said. "'We humbly asked Him to remove our shortcomings.'"

"Asked who?"

"Oh, man," he laughed, "keep coming." He reached into his shirt pocket for his pack of cigarettes. Ritchie was from Iowa but he dressed like a surfer: floral Hawaiian shirts, drawstring shorts that fell past his knees, flip-flops. He was younger than Alex but since he'd been clean longer he'd assumed a kind of protectiveness toward her. Clean time was the great equalizer: three additional substance-free weeks and Ritchie gave her guidance and suggestions, one arm slung around her shoulder like a big brother.

Now he turned to his sponsor, an enormously muscular man with a tattoo of Minnie Mouse on one bicep and Mickey on the other. "Dude!" he said. "Sorry I didn't call last night. I had to scrub the stairs with a toothbrush." Ritchie was living in a therapeutic community and almost every day he underwent some demeaning punishment—a dunce cap when he asked too many questions; a mock-funeral, complete with a coffin and organ music, if he slept late and missed his morning chores—all of which he cheerfully reported at the next day's meeting. His good humor reminded Alex of the guys she and her friends had called "stoners" back in junior high, spaced-out, giggly boys who clustered by the playground swings at lunchtime, rolling joints and ignoring the girls who gazed at them from under the basketball net. Sometimes one of the boys got expelled for stealing forks from the cafeteria, or throwing toilet paper out the window, and then there would be a vigil, with armbands and candles and fervent sobs. "Johnny King didn't do a thing!" Alex and her friends would shout, marching in circles around the school's parking lot, or, "Tommy Slivack, do take him back!"

It was a stage most girls outgrew by high school—a passing fad, like feather earrings and gymnastics. Except Alex had gotten stuck at the vigil, cartwheeling in circle after circle. In fifteen years she hadn't been able to shake her attraction to the stoners, still calling themselves Johnny and Tommy but now scarred from needles and knives, a couple of teeth gone, a couple of kids in Florida or Maine, a couple of years in prison. But the toughness was often combined with a lingering, dogged boyishness—that was what drew her in, the ravaged Peter Pan of it. Billy, her ex-boyfriend, had spent a year in Riker's Island for car theft and liked to sleep on kids' sheets decorated with teddy bears or superheroes.

After the smoking break Ritchie put a hand on her shoulder to steer her inside. Alex heard his sponsor say, "That sucks, man, that toothbrush crap."

Ritchie laughed. "What're you going to do? You try to complain, they pin a diaper on you and stick you in a crib."

Alex was glad she hadn't gotten clean in July; "remove our shortcomings" sounded like a party game, code for strip poker if your parents came home early. But she'd had enough of amends, too. In rehab it was all her counselor talked about. "Clear the wreckage of the past," she'd advise Alex and the other patients in their group therapy sessions. "You're not responsible, but you are accountable." Every night they'd gather in the cafeteria, wearing their blue hospital robes and their blue slippers with the smiley face imprinted on each toe, two dots and a curved line in raised plastic.

"But what do you do if the person you hurt, hurt you first?" asked a fireman who'd been suspended, then later caught shooting heroin in the station's bathroom.

The counselor squinted as if she'd never heard this question, though Alex was sure it was asked each time a freshly aggrieved troupe of addicts were faced with the amends concept. After a moment of concentration she said, "You clean *your* side of the street. *You* do the right thing for the right reason." She sat back, smiling, teeth gleaming white as mints. The first night she'd told them she'd never used drugs, but had been addicted to "things you can't even imagine."

Alex looked at the counselor's shoes, red suede loafers with a delicate heel. Then she looked down at her own feet, the chipped smiley faces, upside-down and frowning. They had taken her shoes when she arrived, along with her Walkman and a copy of *People* magazine. Perhaps these fell into the "things you can't even imagine" category.

She raised her hand. "What if it's for the wrong reason? Then you don't have to do the right thing?"

The counselor sighed and glanced at her watch. Alex hadn't meant to be difficult, but her head felt like it was filled with static; three years of smoking cocaine had short-circuited the synapses, deep-fried the neurons. The other patients called her "Smart-Alex" with a kind of hostile jocularity. They said, "If you're such a Smart-Alex, why are you here?"

"Who said I'm here?" she'd answer. She'd try to laugh, but too much air in her throat and lungs made her cough and then nearly vomit. Most of the time she lay in bed under the thick velour blanket, her arm over her eyes as she focused on her breathing, its stubborn inevitability, until she fell asleep. Then she'd dream about prison, a place she'd never been but pictured as a kind of cafeteria kitchen, with steam and resignation and hairnets.

Billy hadn't talked much about his time there. "I played a lot of handball," he'd say when Alex pressed him. Then he'd smile his breezy smile. He'd been out six months when they met, three years before, and for a long time she suspected that he'd stuffed the agonizing memories into some dark recess, the only thing to be done with the vestiges of such excruciating pain. A couple of years later she realized he was telling her the truth. He'd played a lot of handball.

"And poker, too!" he occasionally added. He was trying to be helpful; he responded to all her questions with a kind of genial compliance. If he was staring into space, she'd prompt, "You're thinking about the prison yard, aren't you?"

"Nah. I'm trying to remember what channel *Scooby-Doo* is on." He'd smile nervously as he glanced at her face. "What do you want? Gang-bangs in the showers?"

She wondered if he saw what she tried to keep out of her eyes: that she wanted *attempted* gang-bangs, and Billy staving off his attackers with a piece of plastic he'd carved down to a blade. She wanted nerve, guts, gristle beneath the pink. She wanted something to offset the Scooby-Doo.

"Nothing?" she'd ask. "No battles in the mess hall? No riots after lights-out?"

He'd tap his head. "I'm sorry, doll. It's just not there." He'd started shaving his head in jail and his skull looked pale and delicate as an eggshell. At night when they lay in bed it would nearly glow, lit up by the headlights of cars outside.

"E.T., phone home," Alex would whisper.

"Now that," he'd sigh, pulling her closer, "was a slamming movie."

They'd met at the Shamrock Pub, where Alex had been bartending since she finished college, a small dive with the stench of smoke and whiskey ingrained in the wood like blood in a carpet. For years she'd meant to go to graduate school—law school, business school, art school; at various times they'd all beckoned. She'd get a picture of herself in a courtroom, holding up a tagged butcher knife with a skeptical eyebrow raised at the jury, or in a Wall Street skyscraper, shouting "bid eight!" or "sell five!" at an assistant, and she'd collect catalogues, set up interviews, even register for the required tests. But each time she got close a fresh idea struck her, making the old one seem stale and ridiculous. "Can you believe I even considered law school?" she said to Peter, the other bartender at the Shamrock. "All those pleas and claims and disclosures. It's like a bad date."

Peter shrugged and poured vodka into a beer stein, one for himself and then another for Alex. She took a sip and opened an art school catalogue on the bar, flipping the glossy pages. "Look at these gorgeous . . . what do you call them, palettes?"

"Twenty thousand dollars," Peter might say, "to draw a couple of hands"—but most of the time he didn't bother to look; he found any sort of ambition, even Alex's half-baked brand, distasteful. He himself despised the Shamrock, he wanted to be an actor, but he didn't believe in headshots or auditions; all that *striving*, he said, was both unseemly and wasteful. Any customer might be a disguised agent, a covert producer, looking to cast a remake of *Ryan's Daughter*; how much more dignified to be discovered by chance. Alex had her doubts about the undercover talent-scout theory—the Shamrock was as glamorous as a parking lot: cracked toilets in the bathroom, and a sign on the front door that said, "Is it not a lonesome thing to be getting old?" But once every few days, when a new face appeared, Peter would don his aggressive Irish twinkle.

The night Billy came in Alex was looking at her newly arrived forestry school catalogue. There was something so peaceful about a vast, cool forest—you could lose yourself for hours without a care. "Look at those gorgeous trees," she was saying to Peter. "That's the true personification of art." Peter couldn't have thought Billy was a film person, with his shiny skull and his flannel shirt and jeans, but covering his bases he said, "We've a hearty lamb stew for supper, if you like," and sent Alex to the jukebox for "Danny Boy." As Alex pushed in the numbers, she'd watched Billy make his way to the bar. She liked the way he walked, a kind of wary, flat-footed stalk. He ordered a Budweiser, shaking his head at the offer of a glass. The melancholy chords of "Danny Boy" came over the speakers and Billy waved Alex over.

"Okay, listen," he'd said. "I need your help."

She took a step back, unnerved by his intensity. "With what?"

"I've got to get my mom a birthday present and I'm stuck. I really really really need your help."

There it was: the undertone of menace—the shaved head, the narrow dark eyes, the gravelly voice—and the boyishness. He was nearly standing on his barstool, bouncing eagerly.

"What are you thinking about?"

"My first idea is a hair-teasing kit."

He had an accent Alex couldn't identify—"idear" and "haih"— something rough that reminded her of kids who cut school to loiter on street corners and drink beer and throw pebbles at cars.

"A hair-teasing kit?"

"You know, when you go to a place and they tease your hair?"

"Like, boy, your hair's a funny color?"

"Yeah. Like, ha-ha, ha-ha, your mama cut your hair with a nail clippers. Not that I should talk," he said, touching his head. "No, seriously: you know how ladies get their hair done, but then they don't want to go to a place for it?"

She pictured a woman standing in front of a mirror with a curling iron, wearing an old pink housedress, a cigarette hanging from the corner of her mouth. There'd be a glass of scotch on the edge of the sink, next to a little jar of bobby pins. She'd always wanted a mother like that, one who shrugged and said *Ah, who the hell knows?* a lot and left you alone. Then she pictured her own mother—at the hairdresser, in a white robe, sipping tea and chatting about the weather.

"They want to do it themselves," Billy was saying. "With a hair-teasing kit."

"To be perfectly honest," Alex answered, sounding more like her mother than she'd meant to, "I have no idea what you're talking about."

But he didn't seem daunted by her tone. "Yeah, join the club." He finished his beer in a gulp, wiped his mouth on his sleeve and grinned, keeping his eyes directly on hers. She bit her lip, staring back, and leaned forward on the bar.

"So," he asked, "you want to do a hang sometime, or what?"

"Do a hang?" They could do this for years, she thought, hold these oblique and indecipherable conversations. She slid her elbows closer to his. It would be like living in a foreign country; she'd be the delicate, refined visitor, a bit taken aback, perhaps, but still fascinated by the natives' customs.

"Hang out." He laughed. "Go to a movie or something."

"All right." She glanced nervously at Peter as she gave Billy her phone number. After Billy left, he said, "Bit of a dodger, eh?"

"Go back to Glocca Morra," she replied. "I like him."

For their first date, Billy had come to her apartment to pick her up. As Alex opened the door, her cat wriggled through her legs out into the hallway. Billy caught her and lifted her into his arms. "You have a kitty-cat!" he exclaimed. He kissed the cat near her eye as she clutched his shoulder. "Oh, I love you, beautiful kitty." He rubbed his chin against her head and the cat began purring loudly, almost hysterically. Billy placed the cat gently on the floor and she rubbed up against his legs. "What a cutie-pie. What's her name?"

"Scarlett," Alex said. She made a face. "I know, but I really wasn't thinking of Scarlett O'Hara. I just liked the name."

Billy was looking around the apartment, his head jerking from the ceiling to the floor to the windowsills. She offered him a drink, to calm him, but he shook his head. "Who's Scarlett O'Hara?" he asked.

Again she had that oddly comforting sensation that they were speaking different languages. "From *Gone With the Wind*?"

The cat had spread herself across Billy's shoes, on her back with all four paws extended into the air. Alex had always envied her, this feline abandon, this innate presumption of approval. Billy reached down to pet her stomach. "Hi, Scarlett. Hi, beautiful," he crooned. He glanced at Alex. "I was locked up for a while. Is it a movie?"

"*Gone With the Wind*?" She nearly shrieked, startling the cat, who rolled to her feet and scurried to a corner table. Had he meant prison? Alex bit her lip and said, "Hm," trying for nonchalance. "Hm: a movie and a book. But they've both been around probably fifty years."

Billy laughed. "You wouldn't believe the sentences they're handing out these days." He leaned against the wall, smoothing his hands down the front of his jeans, then shoving them back in his pockets. "I had a really cool cat, but the day I got sent up she ran away from my mom's, and no one's seen her since."

Alex felt her own hands grow damp and she grasped the sides of her skirt. Somehow she'd wound up leaning against a wall, too, the one opposite Billy, and she was pricklingly aware of this, how symmetrically their bodies were lined up.

"What were you, um, sent up for?"

"Stealing cars. Well, stealing *a* car—the one they caught me with. If they'd caught me with all the cars I'd ever stole, I'd have gotten ten years. But I was kind of fucked up that night." He took a step forward and Alex tensed, but it was toward Scarlett, who yawned and stretched as she sensed his approach. "I shouldn't be telling you this, huh?"

But he didn't seem embarrassed; he was like the cat, rolling onto his back with his limbs spread wide.

"Everyone has something," Alex said, though no *thing*, rivaling jail time, came immediately to mind. "Were your parents upset?"

He snorted. "My dad was in at the same time—he picked a fight with a cop outside a bar. One morning I heard them call my name, which is my dad's name, but I didn't know that at the time. I mean, I knew it was my dad's name, but not that he was there. So I go down to the office and there's my dad, drunk as a skunk."

"What did he say?"

"He's screaming, 'This is my son! Look, everybody, this is my son!' Like he's really proud."

Alex squinted at him, wondering if he was telling the truth. She tried to imagine her father in jail, in his formal business suit with a handkerchief folded into the jacket pocket, greeting her with drunken pride.

"Wow," she said finally. "That's amazing."

He shrugged. "I'll tell you, my mom was none too happy." He bent to the cat and then lifted her into the air, so that her feet were dangling over his head. "You're awesome, Alex," he said. "And you, too, Scarly." The cat stepped down, her nails extended, and lightly scratched his scalp.

"Oh, shit," Billy said. "Is it bleeding?" He dipped his head so that Alex could see. The skin was upbraided with scars, from shaving or something else, she couldn't tell.

"You know what's the worst part of jail?" he said solemnly. He was standing with his back to her, so close she could smell him, talcum powder and cigarette smoke. She shook her head, her heart pounding.

"No Chinese food. You hungry, or what?"

Alex laughed and pushed his back. "No Chinese food? You're crazy, you know that?"

"That's what everyone tells me." He held her jacket for her as she put her arms in the sleeves. "Bye, baby," he said to Scarlett. "It was very very very nice to meet you."

They began seeing each other once a week, then twice a week, then every night. She gave him a key to her apartment. He moved in a toothbrush, first, a razor and a bottle of aftershave; then a few pairs of pants, a pile of flannel shirts, a small teddy bear that he called W and a plastic dog named Clyde, with a spring for a neck that made its head bob. She liked having his things there. She had never lived with a man and the presence of objects was comforting. Billy could not now up and disappear, especially without W and Clyde, to whom he was very attached. He would never just vanish, like so many men Alex had known, without a phone call, without a trace: without, even, a parting shot.

He'd started working for his cousin, painting apartments in Queens and Long Island City, and often he didn't return until late, after Alex had left for the Shamrock. Some nights, by the time she got back, he was already asleep. Scarlett would be lying on the pillow next to him, Billy's hand resting on her back, and Alex would watch them from the doorway for a moment before making her way to the bed, sliding carefully between the sheets and then kissing them both goodnight.

My little family, she'd be thinking.

Other nights, if he wasn't too tired, Billy came to meet her at the Shamrock, but Alex tried to avoid this. It was one thing to watch him from the doorway—her private, swooning heart—but in public Billy could make her squirm. He was unpredictably and oddly whimsical: sometimes he rapped on his skull and said, "Duh!" for no particular reason; sometimes he lectured effusively on the issue of latex vs. oil paint. When Peter saw him come in, he'd narrow his eyes in amusement, much of which was certainly Alex's fault. To downplay the jail angle, which she'd revealed before she gauged her future with Billy, she played up his simpler side, telling Peter all the things Billy didn't know. *Gone With the Wind*, to start, and *My Fair Lady*, and *Rear Window*. Then there was—or really wasn't—Da Vinci and Hemingway.

Eli Whitney, photosynthesis, kiwi.

Continental drift. The placebo effect.

"It's astounding," Alex said. "It's almost awe-inspiring, in a strange way, this vast sea of missing information. It's like a presence in and of itself, what's *not* there."

Peter took a bottle of vodka off the shelf to refill their steins. The Shamrock's owner rarely came in, and when he did he was too drunk himself to remember either Alex or Peter's name, much less notice their state of inebriation.

"So all right, Ms. Mensa," Peter said. "How do you know what Billy doesn't know?"

"Just what I've gleaned." Actually, she'd taken to quizzing him, despising herself all the while but unable to stop.

"Plato?"

"Plato's Retreat? I'll take you there, honey."

"Come on. How about, $e=mc^2$?"

"What do you mean, squared?"

"The shot heard 'round the world?"

"Never heard it."

"You're funny. Okay, 'One if by land, two if by sea'?"

"Nope."

You think there are only two kinds of men, her mother had once said, back when Alex was in high school, dating the stoners. *Dumb and nice, or smart and mean.*

Don't be ridiculous, Alex retorted. *There's dumb and mean, too.*

But Billy was less dumb than culturally oblivious; he had his own set of facts, a different set, stored up and filed away while Alex was in high school, learning about relativity and Paul Revere. How to revive an overdosed heroin addict. How much jail time you'd get for stealing a 1995 Mercedes, a 1976 Chevy, a 1970 Pontiac. How much money inmates received for cooking lunch, for stamping license plates, for digging up coffins at Potter's Field when the bodies, years later, had finally been identified and now required proper burial.

At one of the Eighth Step meetings, Alex heard a woman talk about her husband's drug abuse: he was the real addict, the one to buy the heroin and the needles, the one to tie the scarf around her arm. The woman had a wide-eyed, artfully fragile look, like those girls in grade school who'd coax secrets out of you and then call you a slut behind your back. She said she'd become addicted almost by happenstance, by being in the wrong place at the wrong time. All that had followed—the endless arguments, the stealing, her final call to the cops—was a direct result of that first shot. So who owed amends to whom?

Alex thought of that old joke about the chicken and the egg going to bed together. Afterward, the egg lights a cigarette. "Okay," she says to the chicken. "I guess that settles *that*."

"What you need to decide," Ritchie suggested when Alex told him the joke, "is were you a victim or a volunteer?"

Alex sighed. Everyone made it sound so easy: *victim* behind door number one; *volunteer* behind door number two. Choose the right door and you came out a winner.

"And you don't get to be both," Ritchie added quickly, as if he'd considered this option himself.

One night, a few months after Billy moved in, Alex had come home to find him awake, sitting in the kitchen with his cousin Jimmy. Both still wore their work clothes and were covered in bits of green and black paint. They were celebrating a successful bid on a building in Brooklyn.

"We rocked them!" Jimmy shouted. Alex giggled. She liked Jimmy: he had the same gleeful energy as Billy, and they looked nearly alike, though Jimmy had thick black hair and was several inches shorter.

"What are you up to?" she'd once asked him, over the phone.

"5'6", he answered. "How 'bout yourself?"

On the kitchen table was a journalism school catalogue, covered with several lines of cocaine.

Billy said, "I saved some for you. I know what my girly-girl likes."

"Ooh," she exclaimed, reaching to kiss him as she picked up the rolled dollar bill. "Thank you, angel." She put the bill to her nose and leaned over the catalogue. She'd always liked cocaine, had done it frequently in college when she lived next door to a dealer, a football player who'd sit all day and night on his couch with a huge bag of drugs and a roll of paper towel at his feet. *May I borrow your vacuum cleaner?* Alex would call as she knocked on his door, a neighborly ruse which led invariably to hours of prattle and nosebleeds. But she hadn't done much cocaine since; it didn't seem something one went out to procure for oneself. Once in a while Billy brought it home, a gram or two that Jimmy might pass along, but since cocaine had led him to car theft—sloppy car theft that then led him to jail—he kept their intake to a minimum.

"You guys got a microwave?" Jimmy asked. "We could cook it up." He moved restlessly around the kitchen, turning the sink faucets on and off, pushing the buttons on the blender.

Billy shook his head. "I don't want Alex doing that."

Alex sniffed her second line. Her nose started to itch and she rubbed it, feeling the drip down the back of her throat. "Why not?"

"Uh-uh," Billy insisted. "You don't need to be smoking crack. I don't need to be smoking crack."

"If you smoke cocaine, it's crack?"

Jimmy laughed. "Such a little innocent. Let her try it, Bill."

"I am *not* innocent," Alex protested, though she enjoyed being seen that way. And maybe she was: she'd never before made the cocaine-crack connection. It was like grapes and raisins, or plums and prunes; without being told, she doubted she'd have gleaned the correlation on her own.

"Put it in the microwave, Jimmy. I want to try."

Cocaine had always made her somewhat fearless—*don't you think contact sports are just an acceptable forum for homoerotic expression?* she'd say to the football player. *How many women slap each other on the ass?*—and now she found the ingredients Jimmy requested in a wild rush. "Baking soda? Coming right up. Microwave-safe plate, at your service."

She squeezed Billy's hand as the microwave whirred. She said, "Where's the baby?"

He pointed through the doorway into the living room, where Scarlett lay curled in the basket Billy had bought for her, a miniature cradle with a pink cushion. "She was sleeping on top of the refrigerator when I got home." He smiled; they both took inordinate pride in the cat's slumberous exploits. But the smile faded and he stared at the floor.

"Shit," he muttered. He kicked a pebble of cat litter under the oven. "I've got a not-good feeling about this."

"Aunt Linda will kill me if she hears I let the cue-ball smoke," Jimmy said.

The microwave dinged. "So you guys snort it, and let me smoke it," Alex said. "I just want to see what it feels like."

Victim or volunteer? she thought now, years later, as she sat through one Eighth Step meeting after another. Who said you couldn't be both at once?

When Alex was thirteen, her parents had rented a house a block from the Atlantic Ocean and she'd developed a colossal crush on a lifeguard named Ham. Everything about him dazzled her: how his hair sparkled, like the ocean, where the sun hit it; his tanned and muscled legs; the deep-water blue of his eyes. All summer Alex lay on the sand, her head fuzzy from too much sun and the blaze of infatuation. *I want, I want, I want*, she'd be thinking, though she couldn't have said exactly what—even after she saw Ham's smile aimed at other women, other girls, towels and jellyfish and faraway sailboats.

But with drugs you could say, *I want, I want, I want . . .* and you could get. There was no yearning, no unrequited lust. You sought and you found. You asked and you received. For months after that summer Alex had fantasized about Ham, the blond hairs on his ankles, the silver whistle between his lips. She'd go to school, she'd wash the dishes after dinner, she'd play backgammon with her brother, assuring herself she'd forgotten; and then night would come and she'd lay in bed and spin another fantasy.

Crack offered its own kind of love, made your heart jump and your limbs quiver, as if your veins were funnels and the smoke rocket fuel. It was all those childhood dreams of flying, of pure mindless flight and the world below receding to specks and patches.

Having experienced the downfalls of crack, having experienced jail—even just handball and poker, but *You wouldn't believe the cheating!*—Billy had been less enthralled than Alex. He didn't share her enthusiasm for the accoutrements: the glass pipe and its tiny metal screen, the rocks that were white and filmy as soap chips, how they sizzled when just barely glanced with a flame. He didn't revel in the smell—"burning steak?" Alex would propose, "or is it burning glue?"—or the taste: "Salt water taffy? Marzipan?"

"It smells like crack," he'd answer. "And it tastes like crack."

Though Alex became more voluble the more she smoked, Billy got quiet. He'd listen to her all night, the ramblings and tangents, the recounting of her days in summer camp, in grade school, in high school, even the Ham story and its circuitous relevance. He'd nod and smile as they passed the pipe across the kitchen table; he'd murmur, "This can't be good for the baby," if the cat jumped on his lap, but he'd let Alex push the pipe back at him.

"Just a little more," she'd say. "Then we'll all go to sleep." He'd put his lips to the glass, inhale and exhale, holding his hand over Scarlett's nose.

Sleep, though, became difficult. It could take Alex hours to come down from the cocaine, her whole body twitching randomly—a twinge in her foot, then in her ear, then in her hip—and since she often didn't fall asleep until Billy got up for work, she might not awaken until the next evening. When she wasn't smoking she became fidgety and snide, and after a few months she was perpetually on edge, a combination of withdrawal and exhaustion. At the bank machine, when her cash failed to spit out, she punched the metal slab so hard she nearly broke her hand. At the video store, she berated a customer who cut the line. "For *St. Elmo's Fire*? For that piece of trash, you're in such a hurry?" She made scenes in every shop in the neighborhood, and at the newsstand and the subway token booth. All her life she'd been a good girl, eager to please—a wimp, a pushover, an easy touch—but now when she opened her mouth, everything poured out in an angry river of sewage.

"Who's never heard of Sigmund Freud?" she yelled at Billy. "Who doesn't know at least the first line of *The Star-Spangled Banner*?"

"'I can see clearly now, the rain is gone'?"

She shook her head impatiently. "It starts with 'O.'"

"*Obladi, Oblada*?"

"Why don't you look it up?" She was turning into a mother, a hop-head mother wielding an encyclopedia.

"What's the matter, baby?" Billy sighed. "Missing your glass pacifier?"

She tried to find ways to calm herself: hot baths, yoga, crystals that were meant to circulate peace and spiritual harmony, which Billy flushed down the toilet when they were high. Smoking had started to make him paranoid—"they smell like God," he insisted, flushing and flushing until every last piece of quartz was gone. Some nights, when Alex got back from the Shamrock, he wouldn't even let her speak aloud, in case the apartment was bugged.

Take a hit—quite! he'd scrawl on the back of his hand.

"Quite?"

"Sh! Jesus, Alex!"

At times, even, he suspected the cat. *FBI*, he wrote, or *CIA*, or *IRS*. He pushed her away when she tried to nestle in his lap. If they'd been smoking several hours straight, he dug in her ears and mouth with a Q-tip, trying to dislodge any recording devices. Scarlett began hiding from him, in closets and cabinets, under the couch, beneath the bed. If Billy found her she'd hiss and scratch, and soon his hands were streaked with scars. Some nights she came out after Billy and Alex were asleep, curling up in her litter box, in the pebbles and feces. This was the only time she'd let Billy pick her up, and he'd run the bath, swish her around in the water, and then wrap her in a towel and bring her into bed. He'd place her on Alex's chest and she'd lay half-asleep with the shivering cat in her arms.

"Maybe she likes me again," Billy would whisper, stroking the wet fur. But in the morning, when Scarlett hissed and bared her teeth at him, Alex would have to turn away from the panic in both their eyes.

Amends-recipients, Alex heard at the meetings, didn't necessarily have to be human. Ritchie's sponsor was in the process of making amends to his apartment, repairing the floors that had buckled under the weight of all the stolen stereo equipment he'd stored atop them. A woman talked about making amends to her body after exposing it to bizarre, though lucrative, laboratory experiments. Another woman took on an extra job so she could retrieve the jewelry she'd pawned across the country.

"I kept thinking of each ring and each bracelet alone in the dark," she said, "buried alive in some velvet coffin."

But the most common non-human recipient was a pet. Most everyone who'd had a pet during active addiction had some kind of amends to make. One morning, Alex heard crying outside the church. When she peered out the door she saw Ritchie in his sponsor's arms, sobbing about the dog he once sold to a drug dealer, when he'd run out of money.

His sponsor was patting his back. "You were powerless," he murmured. "You did what you had to do."

Alex shuddered as she turned back to listen to the speaker. She pictured Scarlett, her little black and gray-striped body, Billy's hand stroking her little back as they all fell asleep. In the end, Alex had done what she'd had to do also, but that didn't make the outcome any easier to live with.

When Billy wasn't around, Scarlett would creep out from her hiding place, shaking the dust off her tail and letting out little bleats and cries. Alex would hold her on her lap and feed her spoonfuls of chocolate pudding, looking into her huge green eyes. They were curved and glassy and blank, reflecting Alex's own eyes; after a while of staring, they seemed full of unspoken emotion.

"It's either him or me," they said.

Or: "Why'd you have to give me such a silly name?"

Or: "Help me, Mommy."

Sometimes she'd close her eyes and imagine the heft of the cat as human weight, a small baby, soon to awaken for a diaper change and a bottle. She imagined Billy as the baby's father, teaching it . . . what? How to dig up bodies at Potter's Field? Then suddenly Scarlett's ears would prick up and she'd open her mouth wide and hiss, a low growl torn from the bottom of her throat, and then she'd race off in the direction of the bed or the closet or a kitchen cabinet. Five minutes later Alex would hear Billy's footsteps in the hallway; the cat could feel his approach from blocks away, a kind of extrasensory warning device.

"Where is she?" Billy would demand, and then spend half the night hunting for her, trying to lure her out of her hiding place. He'd get on his hands and knees and peer under the radiator, he'd search the closets, he'd toss toys with tinkling bells into the air. "Here, kitty," he coaxed, glaring at Alex as if she'd instructed the cat to act this way, "Daddy's home, Scarly-pie."

Alex would sit on the couch, smoking as she watched him. "Don't look at me like that," she said one afternoon. "You're the one who stuck the Q-tip up her butt."

"Once!" he protested. "Once up her butt, months ago. And I apologized!"

Finally he gave up and sat next to her, prying the pipe from her fingers. "Maybe I should turn her into a crackhead. Then she'd need me."

"If you're implying I'm a crackhead, you're mistaken," Alex said, pulling the pipe back. "And if you're implying that I *need* you, then you're egregiously mistaken."

Billy dropped his head in his hands. "Can't you for once speak English?"

Most nights he now spent at the bedroom window, perched on a broken stepladder he'd found in the back of the kitchen closet, inspecting the street through binoculars. Some nights, the back of his head was lit up like a barber-pole, blue red blue from the flash of a police car downstairs into which men in handcuffs were being shoved. "Amateurs," Billy would scoff. "Pliers on a Chevy. Christ." With his eyes shining and his jaw clenched, the sweat gleaming on his forehead, he looked restless and fierce and half-crazed. He hardly slept, and when he did, he woke up every hour drenched in sweat, shouting something that sounded like "Folly! Folly!" though in the mornings he insisted she'd been dreaming.

"I don't even know what that means. Maybe I was saying, 'Billy! Billy!'" There were dark shadows under his eyes. Tension seeped like acid from his pores as he told Alex stories about his life before he'd met her. The winter he lived on the streets of Ozone Park, wearing four pairs of socks, three sweatshirts, two pairs of jeans—every piece of clothing he owned—his hair and beard grown out to his shoulders. The summer under the Whitestone Bridge in the Plymouth he'd stolen, nothing to eat but potato chips. "Three months before I touched a bar of soap," he said, "One sniff and you'd have puked."

"I would've held my nose."

"Believe me, sweetheart. Even the other homeless guys wouldn't come within fifty feet."

Sometimes she'd shut her eyes to listen harder, thinking she heard a measure of pride in his voice, and something else underneath, some whisper of nostalgia, and she'd feel a drop in her stomach. Surely he was happy here: she could feel the tenderness in the way he settled Scarlett on her chest, in the way he stroked her cheek, and then Alex's.

Surely he loved them, except watching his face as he talked, she couldn't shake her apprehension.

He missed the life he'd had before her. He missed it the way people who've been cured of a long, lingering illness miss being sick: unaccountably, inconceivably, but there it was.

"Did I tell you about the time I was so fucked up I stole a hearse?" Billy would ask, his lips against the edge of her ear so that the words felt like a hum. "Seven years of bad luck. But that was seven years ago," and then his fingers trailing down her hip drowned out any other sound, the call of the car alarms outside in the night, and the thump on the bedroom floor as the cat hit the ground running.

At the end of May, he'd met her at the door in his underwear, pointing frantically at his thigh. In black ink he'd written, *Scarletts Gone.*

"What are you talking about?" Alex demanded. "Gone where?"

He put his hand over her mouth, quietly closing the door behind her. "I looked everywhere," he whispered. Alex ran to the kitchen; each cabinet was open, bottles of cleaning supplies scattered across the floor. In the bedroom the bed was pushed away from the wall, covered in shirts and pants and shoes.

"Did you check the hallway?"

He nodded. "I'm going to look outside," he mouthed.

"Fuck, Billy. No one's listening." She grabbed a sweater off the bed. "Put on your pants, already. Let's go."

"No, no," he whispered. "You stay here, in case she comes back." He took the sweater out of her hands and dropped it on the bed. Alex watched him as he stepped into his jeans and sneakers and then bent to tie the laces. He'd stopped shaving his head and the hair was growing in patches, thin blond tufts as fine as cotton.

Over his back, she glanced into the living room. She saw the cat's eyes, gleaming, far beneath the couch.

Then Billy stood up and she was looking into his eyes. For a moment, they slid to the side, away from hers, and she thought she saw something shrewd in them, something he didn't want her to see. But when he looked back he was grinning, running his hand over his scalp. "Does this stubble make me look like a retard?"

She shook her head and smiled weakly. "You're not a retard."

"I didn't ask if I am one. I asked if I *look* like one." He made a fist and knocked it on his head. "Duh, Alex."

She'd felt an old rush of affection. She said, "You don't have to do this."

He kissed her quickly and went to the door. "Gotta find the baby," he'd called from the doorway. "We'll be back before you know it."

After he left, she'd put their clothes away and lay down on the bed. A few minutes later the cat jumped up and fell asleep across her legs. Alex waited, watching her, the two of them surrounded by Billy's toys. *Their little family*. She whispered, "I hope you're happy now," and when the phone didn't ring, when Billy didn't come back, she realized she'd meant not just Scarlett, or herself, but Billy, too.

She wanted to believe it: that the flash she thought she'd seen in his eyes had truly existed; that he'd known the cat was under the couch, but he'd needed to go, the lure of the streets so potent he would gladly leave his life behind.

That at least in the moment he walked out the door he was happy, as relieved as she was.

Because then all that had followed—that he'd ended up back under the Whitestone Bridge, and that she'd ended up in in one church basement after another—was as much his fault as hers.

We were near a colossal sign which read PRISON INMATES WORKING. I didn't see any, and I wondered if they just meant in general, somewhere. "Want an ice cream?" he asked, thumbing in the direction of his trunk. (Lamb-Shapiro, page 167)

Pencil Drawings

Christoph Heemann

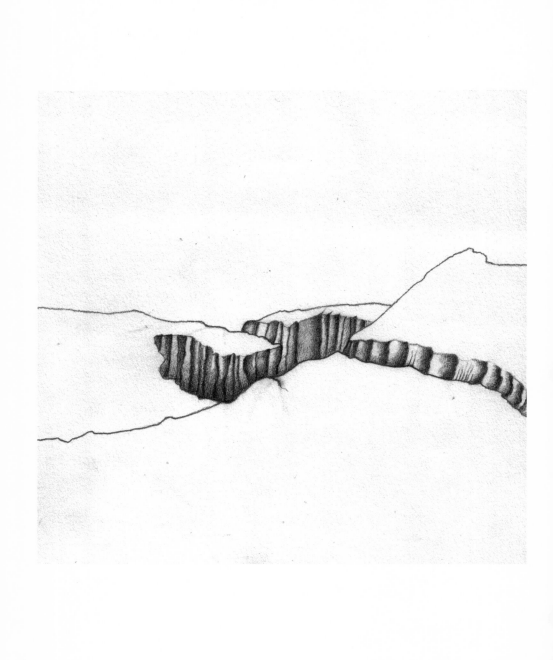

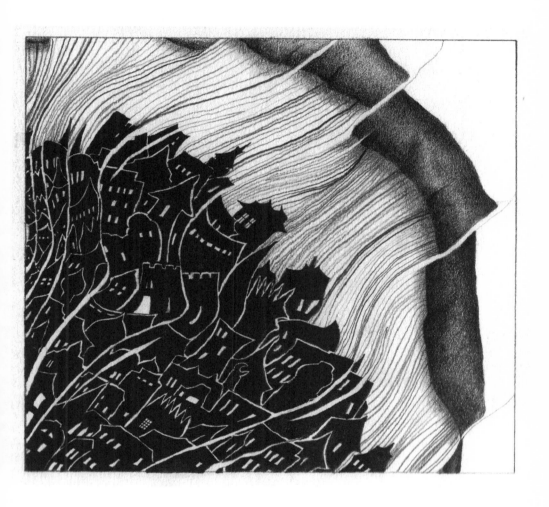

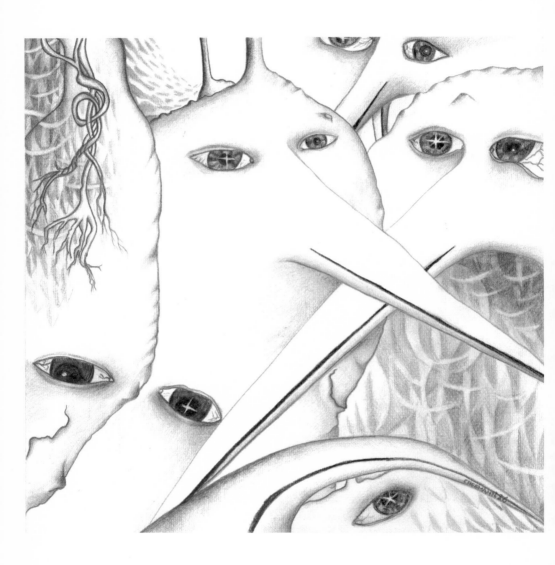

A Drop in the Bucket

Jack Fitzgerald

"NO, I WAS HERE AT EIGHT".

"The hell you were. If you had been it would figure that you'd have been see'n me, and likewise, I would'a been laying eyes on you," said the old man.

He absently scratched at the gray stubble on his chin, and glared down at the boy. It struck him that the boy was getting taller. He could see marks on the boy's face that would be there for good. They would change with him but never leave. It seemed strange to him to notice such a thing.

"So what that comes down to is that you weren't here at no eight A.M. If you were you could have got those sap buckets thawing and stoked up the fire there under the boil-down tubs. Or split up that dry pine in the back like I told you yesterday."

It would be warm again today. The early spring air was rich and clean. Sunlight blazed down on the wet snow, which lay melting between the tall maple trees. The sun was bright and warm but in the tree's shadows it was dark and cool. It smelt like ice.

The old man continued. "So look here now, it's half past nine. I ain't had no second coffee. The ashes are cold and we're just now getting the water out'a that sap."

"Look, boss man, I was here. Me, my arms, legs, hands, whole damn package here ready to work."

"So why them coal buckets colder than that six-pack of mine lying on the floor?"

"Well, hell boss, I didn't know what had become of you. I was bout to get going out my own self when I heard all three cylinders of that old shit-box Ford of yours come fire up."

"Boy, don't you get started in on that truck again. She liable to get a negative sort notion in her bout your arms legs and whole package."

"Shucks ain't scared. Take more than three cylinders to hurt me."

"Lord in heaven boy. Get the hell out and start round'en up. Sun's been beat'en on the east ridge all this wasted morning. Get gone, and bring me back somethin to put over this fire here. Take old Trout, he been nothing but restless all night."

Trout, the big black lab, stood and walked to the doorway, watching the boy with happy but impatient eyes.

The snow sat deep where it had drifted against the trees' thick trunks. It lay heavy and wet in pockets where the ground sheltered the wind. The boy's rubber boots slipped and plunged through the snow as he walked among the trees, gathering their sap. Trout walked with him, following the sharp smells that blew through the spring air. Trout also kept his nose out for the boy; he circled back every few minutes to keep an eye on him.

The boy and the black dog had known one another a long time. The boy didn't know the dog's age nor did the dog know the boy's. Trout knew the boy lived along the road he and the old man sometimes walked in the evening. This was the second spring the boy and the dog had gathered the sap together, so to Trout it seemed familiar and natural. It was in Trout's nature to keep an eye on the boy; as it was in the boy's to talk and call to the dog as he would to any friend.

"Could have backed me up down there, partner." Mumbled the boy, "I known you heard me breaking the ice out of these taps early on."

Trout sat in the snow and watched the boy empty clear sap from a can into a big five-gallon bucket, and then replace the can below a tap board into the maple.

"That old man's drunk himself too much again and gone over sleep'n. I told him I been here at eight."

The boy threw a snowball, Trout caught it in his mouth and bit it. They moved on to another maple along the ridge and repeated the process. Below them the old man spit and carried cordwood into the sugar shack. Soon a blanket of gray smoke rose and hung over the valley.

The morning wore on into afternoon. The boy steadily gathered the sap. As each pail filled, he walked them down the ridge and stacked them in lines along the dirt road. He was wet up to his knees, at times the sap splashed and his fingers were sticky from the sugar.

The wind picked up. It blew in clouds that soon covered the morning sun. It blew through the boy's ragged coat, which was too big, and had once belonged to a father he once had. The wind chilled the sweat on the boy's body and turned the wet snow hard and icy. Trout flapped his ears and sat on the windward side of a tree, he watched the boy collect the last of the buckets.

"God damn, turned bitter on us today didn't it pal," said the boy, rubbing Trout's ears.

They hopped a snow bank and slid down to the road. The boy absently brushed at the crusted snow on his wool pants and chest, but it had hours before turned to ice.

"We got to get up around some of that warm fire, boy". But Trout was already yards ahead loping around the first bend in the road, back toward the warm cabin.

The boy worked the cold out of his toes. They felt much stiffer walking on the hard road then they had in the woods. After the first bend he could smell the fire and the sweet smoke from boiling sap. The clouds overhead were darkening in the late afternoon. It would be snowing again soon.

The old man met him at the open door of the shack. It was hot inside. The fire burned bright.

"How many we end up with out there for today?" Asked the old man. He was drinking beer and had a long iron poker in his hand that he occasionally jabbed into the burning logs.

The boy thought. "We got twenty two buckets and about a half," he answered.

The old man thought a minute then, two. "So that's one hundred ten gallons with change?"

"Yep, that's right." The boy had already figured this out. He figured it one pail at a time while he worked.

"Well, that's good, damn good. That'll give us out pretty near ten gallons of syrup when we get her all boiled down."

The boy nodded, he'd figured this out as well.

The old man took a long pull on his beer. He tossed the empty can into the fire. "OK then, let's get on out before this light starts fail'n. We bring'm back an keep boil'n. I got some venison left from that ten pointer I took in the fall. We can throw on a few steaks for dinner when we get back."

The boy nodded. He was hungry; his stomach had stopped growling hours ago. He'd had nothing to eat the day before.

The old man grabbed his coat off the wall and they headed out in to the gathering evening. The weather had turned very cold. Snow had begun to fall and the wind was blowing harder. They walked down a path cut in the snow, toward the old man's truck, parked on the road. The truck started on the third try, coughing and blowing thick smoke. The boy was right. It only had three cylinders left. But he was too tired to say anything.

By full dark they had gathered all the sap buckets the boy had left along the road. They drove back toward the shack slowly so as not to splash them much. In the warmth of the shack, the old man threw two thick venison steaks on the fire. The boy watched them cook, and his mouth watered. The old man cracked another beer. He didn't know the boy hadn't eaten the day before.

"Morrow ain't going to be no good, Bud. This cold weather, them trees going to harden up. They ain't going to give out no more sap for a day or two, till the sun gets back on'em, loosens them up again. You welcome to come on down help me boil morrow, but we ain't going to get nothing new for a couple days," the old man forecasted.

"No, no thank you. I got a lot up round the house I should be taken care of."

"I understand, but you change your mind, wouldn't mind have'n you."

They sat in silence for a few minutes, listening to the wood pop and crack in the fire. Shadows grew and danced up the walls. Wind and snow rattled the tin roof over head. The old man stood and turned the steaks.

"How things been going up there anyway?" he asked.

The boy shrugged, and watched the fire.

"I ain't seen your ma's car out there in a week or more seems." The old man pressed a little. "She gone on back down to Concord again?"

"Yeah, she say she got some work down there. She say she'll send up some money for the girls soon."

The old man nodded. He was old but not so old. He knew the kind of work she had found in Concord. "Think'en that venison should be done. Hell if it don't smell as good as the day I shot it," said the old man.

He opened another beer and handed the boy a plate. They ate together in hungry silence with Trout watching from the fire. When they had finished, the old man stood and poked at the fire a time or two with the toe of his boot.

"Well son, we did good today. This cold weather ain't going to last long. Soon that sap go'en to be just pouring out of all them trees. What we figure for today, about ten gallons of syrup?" he pulled out his wallet and began counting. "So that'll bring one hundred and twenty in town when all's said and done. And like a told you, you got a third in all this so here's forty. Square?"

"Yeah, we are. Thank you much," said the boy standing and taking the money.

"Thank you. OK, I'll run you on home. It's on the way and it's get'en late. But do me a favor, would you. Take them bones there out back, give'm to Trout, then throw a couple more logs on the fire and bank her up real good. I'll meet you out in the truck." The old man lit a smoke and walked out into the night.

The boy did like the old man asked. He liked to feed Trout, but tonight he was in a rush. It was getting late and he was worried about both his little sisters who had been home alone all day.

When he had finished with the fire he got his coat and walked quickly down to the truck. The old man was there; the bed was half full with spilt cordwood. The old man spoke up before the boy could ask.

"Look, I'm going to lend you some here wood to get you all through this last cold snap. You can pay me back at the end of the year. I'll take it out of you, don't you worry. You can cut me some green wood come summer. Here's some meat for them sisters of yours back at the house, too. I got more than I can eat here; that buck was a fat son-of-a-bitch. So don't you say no." He handed the boy a thick paper-wrapped package of venison.

The boy nodded and looked down at his boots. "Thanks boss man. I appreciate that."

It was cold and dark in the house when the boy arrived home.

Mandy sat braiding Tabitha's hair. They were cold and sat together under an old quilt. They looked up and smiled at him when he walked in, kicking snow from his boots. He was proud of his sisters then. They didn't first ask him to start the fire, nor did they whine and ask where their mother was. The boy no longer felt tired or sore when he saw his little sisters. He grew and felt stronger. He split the wood in back of the house, and carrying it to the small stove his fingers did not feel sore or cold or dirty. And his sisters clapped and laughed when the flames started to rise.

In Place of an Introduction

Assembled by Honor Moore

Wind-ridden, running slantwise against / its seaward urge.[1] A lodestar . . . above a gray / page of snow.[2] Please refrain from talking . . .[3] talk with tears.[4] It's the yearning she can't seem to abide. She of slim skirt . . .[5]

As if you never escaped that house: / as if you weren't free.[6]

What do they not see?[7] took off thick glasses . . .[8] half feeling / for the first time, a brilliant tinge of wickedness . . .[9] from which ambiguity would be banished . . .[10]

A dozen rivers more underlie the city / if you believe the oldest citizens.[11]

Although he was a god what could he do?[12] That might have been seen as breaking the surface / Still we leaned quite far forward . . .[13] Take the polished stillness from a locked church . . . [14] the door to the room across the hall is always open.[15]

Ooh[16]! I see it in the reticent / curve of his neck.[17]

Can you recount the last three images in reverse order?[18] *Will you stay with me?*[19] A Lockheed Galaxy rattles our sills / through cloud cover. / They are preparing for war again.[20] I am afraid of how Goya saw the world . . .[21]

OPEN CITY

Even needled trees reflect the slanting light.[22]

Why then is the poet / the last to see as a god / that earth from the heavens is radiant fruit[23]? But, buried in the dust of too much, who / Will hear the man cry out[24]? I bending over you— / both of us straining to see without glasses . . .

united in the grammar of common / longing, reaching back, together . . . [25]

1. Richard Matthews (page 107)
2. Joanna Klink (page 109)
3. Robert Polito (page 111)
4. Tom Healy (page 113)
5. Susan Wheeler (page 115)
6. Suji Kwock Kim (page 117)
7. Fanny Howe (page 119)
8. Joan Larkin (page 123)
9. Cynthia Marie Hoffman (page 125)
10. C. K. Williams (page 129)
11. Kirmen Uribe, translated from the Basque by Elizabeth Macklin (page 131)
12. Daniel Mark Epstein (page 135)
13. G. E. Patterson (page 137)
14. Carolyn Forché (page 139)
15. Semezdin Mehmedinovic, translated from the Bosnian by Ammiel Alcalay (page 141)
16. Eileen Myles (page 143)
17. Donna Masini (page 145)
18. Elizabeth Willis (page 147)
19. Jill Bialosky (page 149)
20. Peter Gizzi (page 151)
21. Victoria Redel (page 153)
22. Julia Bolus (page 155)
23. Jane Miller (page 157)
24. Eamon Grennan (page 161)
25. Peg Boyers (page 163)

Hudson

Richard Matthews

      Wind-ridden, running slantwise against
its seaward urge, corkscrewed below the park-
capped sewage plant, it flattens, olive
      to steel-blue, past the red lighthouse, broadens
beyond the brace of the Palisades—the bridge

      confused with haze—still far from the disillusion
of freshwater, almost promising again
to open a passage west into the East.
      You could have walked on the teeming shad
once where present callery pears and shadblow

      root in manufactured land. I stand
near their blizzard shade, by a broken
viewfinder, not serving, not waiting,
      not even standing it: the manicured beds,
my illusion of hands, of malleable days.

      Those sheets of diabase, the opposite
shore . . . A late-night jingle for its old
amusement park keeps coming back: *all day
      and after dark, get cool in the waves
of the pool, come on over* . . . Come on then.

OPEN CITY

   The accidental north, its white-stunned,
cry-consuming cul-de-sacs, haunts
the edges of our cartography. Orient, half,
   full, occulted, increscent, blue: I will cross
by whatever moon they give me tonight.

Lodestar

Joanna Klink

A lodestar held lightly in the sky above a gray
page of snow. Someone speaks a word
and the boats are born to time, trailing out against the ice.
And we judge this valuable—weather undone across a field,
the boats soft black discs upon the whitening water.
And the heat that forms within our throats
as we stand and look out. Who are you, next to me?
To shine in unawareness like the ice at night on the field.
To say the only thing you want—boats below a lodestar,
and in another country, beyond a gray wave of snow.
Late afternoon in our eyes, and somewhere a girl
sitting in a chair, emerging from thought or
preparing a future. Seeds float through the air
beneath a fire maple—it is late in the day or it is
autumn. Someone brings me a newspaper
—it is you. Had I understood what portions
would be lost or made solid by the pressures of such
emptiness. The lodestar rises each evening in winter,
mute in its ripping distance, and the fire maple
drops a few leaves in the casual winds. Further out,
someone says a word into the summer air
and a bird emerges from the lawn's warm shadow,
a deep gray spread across the northern sea
where boats form a slow nomenclature of movement,
and everywhere we look out upon a darkness whose scarcity
we cannot comprehend. You are always nearby
and I turn to you or touch you. And in the ports already

the shipbuilding has begun, men tugging at steel
through the clear blows of metal.
We watch them as though through water,
involved as we are in the unaccomplished,
and a cold film of ocean is swept into sky—
seagulls resting against the liquid light, the fringe
of a crowd drawn, like us, to stare midway into sea,
into a field I have tried for so long to pull
free from. How remote the months between us,
the slight glow of our bodies in these rooms, a few words
that hold their sound across the stillness of hours.
You feel a star in its private heat above a field,
a woman curled into sleep or walking among the long
bars of shadow-trees through which pour shining
coins. To each belong the corrections of light,
the suffering that shall not heal, the singing that lifts
—washed, unwinged—from a small boat at sea.

Please Refrain from Talking During the Movie

Robert Polito

When I can't make you understand I repeat myself
I repeat

If you don't stop asking me all these questions how
Will I understand anything

Please refrain from talking during the movie

I need a life that isn't just about needing
To escape my life

Please God please may Carrie please fall for me

I want to show off my hidden camera
I'm an informer but I have my limits

You hurt him once before now what
If she's there I don't know if I can go

Please refrain from talking during the movie

Leave a message if you can't reach me
To exit press enter and don't forget your receipt

When I think I read new things I want
A life where I read and think new things

OPEN CITY

Please refrain from talking during the movie

I want to know nothing
Again

Please God please may Carrie please fall for me

I repeat myself when I can't
Make you understand I repeat

What the Right Hand Knows

Tom Healy

A city of listeners sleep muffled
under dust in one of my ears.
I didn't know they were missing

until forty months into things
shutting the fortress gates
of my hands against both sides

of everything outside.
I needed to hide from my voice
too old to hear it talk with tears.

One of my hands slipped—
to nothing. I listened
and realized only the other

controlled what was: the sound
of the world switched off
and on leaning on my elbow.

It was the thrill of vandalism,
a game I called Break the Noise,
a secret of my grand imperfection.

Voices still reach everyone
living within me only by singing
on my left. I offer this in explanation

of rumors the moon's dark side
has no sound, and why so many
whispered comforts run off

stage right, frightened by
the Buddha I've sent to guard
those of my cities lying to the east.

Barry Lyndon in Spring Lake, 1985

Susan Wheeler

Benched by the duck pond, he talks about book learning,
swinging his leg on the other, back, forth: diffident in her rage.
And you cannot help overhearing—her tirade, his wheedling replies.
It's the yearning she can't seem to abide. She of slim skirt.

You're done for the day, done and diminished, and the lap
of the pond on its laughable bank won't drown out the shop of his voice.
This man Barry's blind eye for figural blight. The girl reads,
Debtor to your dunner or debtor to death. Book learning.

The LED ticker's impervious to the numbers on its regular lappings.
The girl wads her hair in her fist and releases.
Ditch the story and give us the green.

Greens of the willow, the black maples, the viburnum. Your own bench,
greened in its molds. Green of her T-shirt, green of cold gazes,
Barry goes green under solid regard. Copper pennies, oxide greened.

He's up now and swaying, he's round the pond circling.
Under the browning sky a crow swoops and lands.
He unlooses his watch, he stoops to the bank, he slits with his hands
the shore's green muck. Muck-monger, Barry and his body
follow his hands, slip under the water giving gravity sway. Ducks
shuffle. And the water casts him full back upon shore.

The cylinders of the rotary press impressed the strips from which farthings
were cut, in the Hall in Tyrol. Oh for Chrissakes. Join the human race,

give up the glitz, the snow, what can it be worth, the society you buy?
I don't need Lacroix, you don't need foie gras. Come back to earth
where it's school clothes that call. He: failure of imagination,
gray and scint, that scolds the projected bounty; his: failure to drown.
Despair to denigration, him, now that he's aground. He waves
his loathing back and forth, and the object of it morphs.

You've a prototype in hand, you're an inventor, you've got a transformer
to sell as a toy. Your day's been a hard one courting the money,
hoi polloi with muck-hills high as the trees, and in the summer evening
on the still village green it's peace and reprieve that you need,
not a farce of the debtor deranged by his debts, the enabler enraged and
the pond ducks stirred up. Your briefcase will pillow your head.

Supply the supply side, the slop said.
Power to the people. And the pea brains perk up.
You will have a windfall soon. Lucky numbers: 8, 8, 8, 18.

He has rent his wig. Torn his toupee. The woman turns in green shame.
Barry, gleaming, steps from the green into the lane, gait dogged by honking:
LeBaron screeched to a halt that lurches, growling, when Barry is by.

I put my hand upon my heart and, there, felt naught but need.
You were in invention's up-tick then, but this you could not know.
Lie on the ties of the eighties track: and this, I did.
No crow swooped which tallied more than contrivèd need.

Aubade Ending with Lines from the Japanese

Suji Kwock Kim

The sound of wind hissing through muslin curtains
wakes you from a nightmare of childhood—

parents shouting at each other, someone smashing a whiskey bottle
on someone's skull, a door slamming

for good. As if you never escaped that house:
as if you weren't free.

Outside the sun slanting through palm trees
dazzles, hurts, with the painful sweetness of things that can be loved

only once: not so much that time passes,
but that love does, passing *into* me, the way light would

if it could glitter through drifting hair and seep into the brain beneath
to stain it in a way both of and beyond

myself, until it burns away what I was, what I meant
to become. My eye is peeled.

Facing the music, if it is music *(Did you mean
what you said? What will you do next? Is it too late?)*

I know I'll never know another home,
fumes of jasmine, ripgut-brome rifting our dreams of happiness

and our real happiness, the one we didn't mean
to feel, and may or may not recognize in time.

The autumn wind is blowing;
we're alive and can see each other, you and I.

The Plan

Fanny Howe

I am going to follow Brother
into his dream
The light is good there
for staring

I can scan the horizon
and bend its lens
from my own
left turn to its

I know my atheism
is intact in Brother's
dream—protective in fact
it comforts him

Eyeless stars wink
in our shelter
on a wide plateau
ringed by roaring elms

What do they not see?
No roof, no rule
But Brother and me
standing separately

A Reach

Fanny Howe

One summer we were together
all the time
But you didn't love me

Only called my name to come
and take you home

A person can know love as wanting
and un-had
and be unable to leave

Which one of us was wrong
to go forward anyway
with all our understanding?

*

Through the apple trees
I saw the children blow away the light
between the greens
reach down
and not eat a bite.

*

Who were you with
when I wasn't there

Crazy idea
at my screen door

Blooded-up by fingers?
Hard-happy?

Against what back and knee?

You me
turned away from

but don't explain your position
Its absence was mine

Full Moon Over Brooklyn

Joan Larkin

He never saw the platinum
world hung in the upper right
corner of her kitchen window
flat as Earth in an old book

but rushed toward it past the graveyard
carrying gin and African daisies
past horns hooting and kids
shouting their nightly litany of *faggot*

felt its pull
where Ocean Ave met the Atlantic
Pressed her doorbell set dogs barking
took off thick glasses then shoes

as she undid his belt and the tide
in her small house of water turned

Dear Commercial Street,

Cynthia Marie Hoffman

One trembles to think of that mysterious thing
in the soul, which seems to acknowledge no human
jurisdiction, but in spite of the individual's own self,
will still dream horrid dreams, and mutter unmentionable things.
   —Herman Melville

On this my fifth day in Provincetown I have discovered your cabinet of
   knives,
cleverly enough tucked away in the furthest room of your most crowded
   retail store.

What's more (also clever), you've backed it with a mirror
so that when I stand and gape, I am as well looking past the knives

and into myself. I know this must sound crazy, but
I imagine the palm of my hand pushing through the plate of glass

which is the only thing that separates us, the way one child
pushes another child in the chest, half joking, half feeling

for the first time, a brilliant tinge of wickedness. Already
I hear the clatter the glass would make. The almost inaudible

screech of steel passing through the heavy collarbone
and the first row of the shopkeeper's ribcage. The final puff of air

whistling through his mustache hairs. Why are you trying to hide from me?
Commercial Street, I bid you consider my virgin hands.

I wake up in the bed where the man I wake up to swallows in his sleep
and I am witness to the miracle of the clenching pharynx. Commercial
　　Street,

you must recognize the fact that I am fully awake when I look at this man
and see myself ripping the lump from his throat.

There is no question I am capable of it. There is no question
that my fingers retain in them the memory

of puncturing the earth in my mother's garden
and exiting the hole with the bulb of a lily seized.

Or that my fingers would recognize this new act
as akin to digging bulbs out of gardens, and thus

they'd already know, even before my hand took flight for his throat,
exactly how to perform it. Such are the workings of the human mind.

I would like to submit the first piece of evidence. Exhibit A:
The orbital frontal cortex. Digital imaging proves conclusively

that this underside of the brain, located directly over the eye
sockets and behind the brow, is liable to overheat

due to a biochemical imbalance. If you mean to understand me
I say there is a fire set in my skull. Exhibit B: The caudate nucleus,

where winks the conniving little spark that keeps on burning
even as the engine drags its emptied bowels back to the station.

Commercial Street, would you buy it if I said I love that man? And what if
    I admit
I've imagined the stainless steel prongs of a fork going into his left eye

the way a bird's claws pop through the skin of a cranberry?
He has leaned over the crackling banana flapjack batter

and laid his lips behind my ear. Two and a quarter feet away from the
    searing pan.
Only two and a quarter feet, I'll say it again, yet I have done nothing.
    Nothing.

So you can take me, after all, into your most dangerous corridors. In fact,
spill all of your knives out into the street. Have your shops spit them out

from their doors. Set them in my pockets, fill up my purse,
I'll hold as many as I can in my hands. Your men, women, and children
    are safe.

The man I wake up to and I will grow old together. And he will die
before I do. And I will have thought to carry with me his light trench coat

in case the way from the funeral home gets cool. When my turn comes
at the coffin, I will set the back of my hand to his throat delicate as a moth

touching down on a bough. And the last time I ever
turn from him, his coat will still be balanced on my arm.

Why shouldn't you trust me? Commercial Street,
I bid you consider my virgin hands.

The Clause

C. K. Williams

This entity I call my mind, this hive of restlessness,
this wedge of want my mind calls self,
this self which doubts so much and which keeps reaching,
keeps referring, keeps aspiring, longing, towards some state
from which ambiguity would be banished and uncertainty expunged;

this implement my mind and self imagine they might make together,
which would have everything accessible to it,
all our doings and undoings all at once before it,
so it would have at last the right to bless, or blame,
for without everything before you, all at once, how bless, how blame?

this capacity imagination, self and mind conceive might be the "soul,"
which would be able to regard such matters as creation and destruction,
origin and extinction, of species, peoples, even families, even mine,
of equal consequence, and might finally solve the quandary
of this thing of being, and this other thing of not;

these layers, these divisions, these meanings or the lack thereof,
these fissures and abysses beside which I stumble, over which I reel:
is the place, the space, they constitute,
which I never satisfactorily experience but from which the fear
I might be torn away appalls me, me, or what might most be me?

OPEN CITY

Even mine, I say, as if I might ever believe such a thing;
bless and blame, I say, as though I could ever not.
This ramshackle, this unwieldy, this jerry-built assemblage,
this unfelt always felt disarray: is this the sum of me,
is this where I'm meant to end, exactly where I started out?

The River

Kirmen Uribe

There was a time a river ran through here,
there where the benches and the paving start.
A dozen rivers more underlie the city
if you believe the oldest citizens.
Now it's a square in the workers' quarter,
that's all, three poplars the only sign
the river underneath keeps running.

In everyone here is a hidden river that brings floods.
If they are not fears, they're contritions.
If they are not doubts, inabilities.

The west wind has been shaking the poplars,
people barely make their way along on foot.
From her fourth-floor window a grown woman
is throwing articles of clothing.
She's hurled a black shirt, a plaid skirt,
the yellow silk scarf and the stockings
and the black-and-white patent-leather shoes
she wore the winter day she came in from her town.
In the snow they looked like frozen lapwings.

Children have gone racing after the clothing.
The wedding dress exited last,
has been clumsy and perched on a branch,
too heavy a bird.

OPEN CITY

We've heard a loud noise. The passersby have been startled.
The wind has lifted a poplar out by its roots.
They could be a grown woman's hand
awaiting a hand's caressing.

Visit

Kirmen Uribe

Heroin had been as sweet as sex
she used to say, at one time.

The doctors have been saying now she won't get worse,
to go day by day, take things easy.
It's been a month since she failed to wake up
after the last operation.

Still and all, we go every day to visit her
in Cubicle Six of the Intensive Care Unit.
Today we found the patient in the bed before hers
in tears, no one had come to visit, he'd said to the nurse.

An entire month and we haven't heard a word from my sister.
I don't see my whole life stretching before me now,
she used to tell us.
I don't want promises, I don't want repentance,
just some sign of love is all.

Our mother and I are the ones who talk to her.
Our brother, with her, never said too much,
and here doesn't make an appearance.
Our father hangs back in the doorway, silent.

OPEN CITY

I don't sleep nights, my sister used to tell us,
I'm afraid to go to sleep, afraid of the bad dreams.
The needles hurt me and I'm cold,
the serum sends the cold through every one of my veins.

If I could only escape from this rotten body.

Meanwhile hold hands, she implored us,
I don't want promises, I don't want repentance,
just some sign of love is all.

Two poems translated from the Basque by Elizabeth Macklin.

The Jealous Man

Daniel Mark Epstein

Soul-sick, he cannot sleep. Outside,
Hydra, the old dragon of chaos,
Coils across the moonless winter sky.
On its back the Crow and Goblet ride,
Constellations the magi identified
Long ago, sailor, lover, insomniac,
All who have lost, yearned to recover
Their paths. Soon real crows will come
Vexing the dawn with cries, blotting the oak.

Who but a stargazer would have known
The crow was silver once, Apollo's pet
Raven? Then the god in fury cursed
The gossip bird for telling him his mistress
Coronis played him false with a mere man;
Cursed the bird black and shot the fickle woman
With an arrow aimed so neatly through the heart
Even his art couldn't heal her. Better, he thought,
It would have been if he had never known.

The night is long, the tale is not yet done.
Hating himself then, hating the strung bow,
The arrow and the angry hand that notched it,
Although he was a god what could he do?
Drink from the goblet on the dragon's back
For courage, and carve into the steaming womb
Of his dead love, bringing to light his baby boy

OPEN CITY

Who one day with serpent-coiled staff,
Would heal the lame and sick, and baffle death.

G. E. Patterson

wide   wide

"... Emma ..."   "... Paul ..."
   —Charles Darwin   —Norman Mailer

wide wide

Drift
Land

I think it never evaporates

Indeed there were planes to your mild surprise
Before you had known what it was you wanted
That filled rooms with a kind of happiness
Then there were many possibilities

So it could be you thought the way it was
Thinking of the first time we turned away
You went in awed in the hope it would help
Whatever it was that was about to happen

We thought we had something and let it go
The world had shown you how it could be done

That might have been seen as breaking the surface
Still we leaned quite far forward to see if
It was true over time that you'd feel nothing
Ever after could be this beautiful

Refuge

Carolyn Forché

In the blue silo of dawn, in earth-smoke and birch copse,
where the river of hands meets the Elbe.

In the peace of your sleeping face, *Meine Leibchen.*

We have our veiled memory of running from police
dogs through a blossoming orchard, and another

Of not escaping them. That was—ago—(a lifetime),
but now you are invisible in my arms, a soul

Acquiring speech, the body its blind light, whispering
Noli me frangere even as it is in death shattered.

We were *one in the other*. When the doves rose
at once, and our refuge became wing-light—

Prayer

Carolyn Forché

Begin again among the poorest, moments off, in another time and place.
Belongings gathered in the last hour, visible invisible:
Tin spoon, teacup, tremble of tray, carpet hanging from sorrow's balcony.
Say goodbye to everything. With a wave of your hand, gesture to all you have known.
Begin with bread torn from bread, beans given to the hungriest, a carcass of flies.
Take the polished stillness from a locked church, prayer notes left between stones.
Answer them and hoist in your net voices from the troubled hours.
Sleep only when the least among them sleeps, and then only until the birds.
Make the flatbed truck your time and place. Make the least daily wage your value.
Language will rise then like language from the mouth of a still river. No one's mouth.
Bring night to your imaginings. Bring the darkest passage of your holy book.

Hotel Room

Semezdin Mehmedinovic

In the hotel, called the Royal Palace for some reason,
The door to the room across the hall is always open.
Calmly lying on the sheets, breath betrays a body there.
I think he's dying. And he knows it.

From the dark room you can hear the cheerful sound of a kid you can't see
And that makes you think it can't be a real voice
But sounds the dying hear before they go
Like an utterance in their very own first attempt at language.

I don't know why hotel rooms seem so endless
To the point I leave with no memory:
Two days and three nights
I traveled from the east to the west coast
And in my weariness I refuse to believe the
Land is any bit smaller than this hotel room

Precautionary Manifesto

Semezdin Mehmedinovic

The fifth night of the journey, the body
Adapts itself to its disconnection from solid ground.
At Mendota Station,
Which in an American Indian language
Means "Fork in the road," a passenger got on

Already explaining why
He wore only a certain kind of jacket:
"Because the thickness of the fabric
Protects me from snake bites."

He, as you might expect, talked slowly
(Every word a precautionary manifesto)
Saying that he was on his last trip,
That, maybe, he'd go to Canada,
But only when everything was covered in ice
And people, understandably, had slown down

Two poems translated from the Bosnian by Ammiel Alcalay.

Ooh

Eileen Myles

Baby's
apricot
with
its
tongue
hanging
out

I fight
the constant

conscious
conscious

I fight
for
you.

3 Card Monte

Donna Masini

They're at it again. On Broadway, the crowd
closes around the dealer, his cards face down in the uncertain
sun. They never win, but they keep

coming back. Last night I slept with him again.
Again the long sexless night. Desire. What sends them
back, what makes them

inch up, into his chants, throwing their burning hard-
earned cash, what propels them
to that table? Is it his beautiful hands, the voice that makes him

luster? It looks easy, a piece of cake. They're sure
to win this time, they must, they can see the trick, the sly
card they have outwitted. Behind them the Tower

Records sign, the cheap eager dresses on racks, the Broadway traffic.
Again and again I go back to him, banging against him,
certain this time he'll . . . yes, this time . . .

I see it in the reticent
curve of his neck, the grief in his stomach. On this kind of corner
I've passed my loneliness, year after year, notebook in hand.

Who would have thought love would come so slowly.
December it seemed a sure thing. I raced into it,
announced myself, the way I've read salmon

leap against a stream,
that awful arc, the way music will build, ache, but release
doesn't come. I love you,

he says. Month after lonely
month I fall for it, fill up with it,
ticking down Broadway, the way those salmon—how do they?—

stupid, lusting, plunging. The crowd scatters
its disappointment, each trying to figure
how he'd lost, it had really looked like,

she'd been certain, it had seemed so certain, a sure
thing, those beautiful hands, that voice, and now
a new crowd begins to form. Face after stupid face.

Ferns, Mosses, Flags

Elizabeth Willis

We all live under the rule of pepsi, by the sanctified waters of an in-ground pond. Moss if it gathers is a sign of shifting weathers, the springing scent of consensual facts. A needle's knowing drops into focus while you sleep in its haystack. A boy on the road, a guileless girl disguised as a brook. Even trees deploy their shadows, embossing your skin with the sound of freedom breaking. No one mistakes choice for necessity. Look at the pilgrims in your filmy basket, illustrious eyebrows colored with chalk. The lake is panicking. A latent mystery detected in sepia is quaking to its end. I too have a family astonished, unsaintly. Asleep, I saw them. A porcelain dome insisting on trust, jeweled with telepathy. I don't know how to pour this country from a thinner vessel. Or account for the era of Martian diplomacy, its cheap labor glossily wigging. Little bridges connect every century, seasonally covered with the rime of empire. Can you successfully ignore the eyes in the painting? Can you recount the last three images in reverse order? I read the picture and did what it told me, ducking through the brush with my tablet and pen, following some star.

Demon Lover

Jill Bialosky

Is it still snowing?
Yes, she said.
Will it go on?
It will blanket the earth.
It will fall
over the hidden valleys and seep
into the bark of the trees.
It won't end, she said.
Will you stay with me?
I won't leave, she said.
I must go then, said the lover.

Take the 5:10 to Dreamland

Peter Gizzi

Sometimes I am so far from myself
the stumble above only makes it worse.
A Lockheed Galaxy rattles our sills
through cloud cover.
They are preparing for war again.

The words come in winter
the steel, the ice petals
and for a moment the world is born of sun—
a Victorian lamp, that Roman campfire,
an Edison bulb at the Smithsonian.

The heart's compass is never surer
than late snow and rustic branches.
It's a shame sunsets are such a knockout
so early in the century.

The distance is keening and sharp with tears.
This distance is loose wire free of its mooring.

O Lady of Czechowski
when I am home in my early bed
and the clouds begin to blush
I hope you'll answer the prayers
of those calling to you.

OPEN CITY

The green of night is upon the door.
Today a girl asked if doves
blow into old bottles to call to us.
Small things are what prey upon sleep.

The Palace of Weep

Victoria Redel

Take that I am afraid of how Goya saw the world.
Take that I love Goya and his dark invention of my life.

My life is the invention of all women waiting on West Side stoops
happy for an iced coffee before picking up kids.

I cannot sleep at night for the chimney sweeps who live in Blake.
Blake and Goya ignite in this city's children, their doses of asthma, plastic
prizes for cindered bronchia, the chemical twitch and Ritalin fretting.

I think I have everything except keys which I am always losing.
I have the squashed hope of every showy failure before us.
The signs on cars plead our criminal efforts: trust me I have nothing.
When a siren stops in this city, people worry.

Take my hope for the palace of the unconverted, the stumbled
offers of the confused, the stalled recovery of each morning
but not the freon steam cleaning another hole in our thin universe.

This is 79th Street where wind is our hero.

Take the double-parked, GOLDEN KEY 580-0066,
24-Hour Emergency Service. Take the locksmith
who walks—belts, tools and a chalky damp jumpsuit—
straight through an afterschool melee of mothers and children.

OPEN CITY

Let's drift together up the tipsy raft of Broadway
bannered with the bedazzled prayers of every generation.
Leave for a next true world the boy who runs
out of school and up into my arms.

I want more Goya. I want more July. "I want my mother,"
moans a little girl. So the boy answers, "It's okay. You can share mine."

Clasp

Julia Bolus

I'm giving you all my nothingness.
        —Edward Hirsch

I.
Your letter returned unopened.
I saved it that way. A year later your
birthday, unmarked. Winter coming. Don't think
of this as silence. Remember
the notebook you kept?

II.
He scatters me with his touch—gold fingers
through green velvet. Grasses going amber.
Even needled trees reflect the slanting light.

His sleeping face: Michelangelo's dying
slave. I dream we sleep in an old farmhouse,
walls washed white, white curtained
windows. A door swings open
or closed—spiral stairs, shadows.

He's driving. I ask him about heaven
and hell. Turning, he says: *I think
there's heaven in every moment.*

OPEN CITY

III.
I gathered everything, before learning
the rules of places they would keep you.
Here, earth's crammed with heaven.
Now I understand nothing
can be saved. I'm saving it all for you.

---

earth's . . . Elizabeth Barrett Browning

From A Palace of Pearls

Jane Miller

9

I'm going to see what I can see

whenever it flashes

in the night sky fighter jets practice

won't their metals attract lightning they appear not to move Jesus

the shadow leaks out of the thing like a fluid but has no relation

to real shadow perfect and perfectly unreflective

is it bloody

I'll call it an accident

that way there can be no relief no foreboding all event

NO ONE WILL BE RESPONSIBLE LEAST OF ALL

22

My darling would rather raise a goose

before she'd cook and eat it

does that mean she would then eat it

is not such ambiguity

a creamy golden cherry blushing

impenetrable all clear juice and perfume

of honeyed lavender Michelangelo's males

don't have more porcelain beauty than my white peach

my beloved can separation return us

our young and lithe marriage our heroics of love

where I pull back the pale green summer coverlet

upon the manner of our incompleteness a blue

which may not exist in nature and a gray too

beyond our understanding but often present

to find willingness and open air and grandeur

as the sun and the moonlight variously play

upon our round bruised bodies and our bruised sharp minds

our hope seems justified but let us not return

to innocence let us come with half-closed eyes

to feel more powerfully actual than merely real

things stomachs taut with sexual thunder rumbling

some moments of some days at home in our own bed

and live the rest of the time in this great rotten country

trying to make sure there is a rest of the world

it's no example to fathom a banquet of fruit

squeezed and dripped nimbly in the sealed wild

mood of eager mind my darling loves me

unaccountably despite my wasting her time

in this poem while she's hard at work in the real world

of Rome and I'm at home excoriating

a surface a small matter never mind it feels

like my own skin unheroically grating a lime

in God's hands but more ironically than some

Renaissance painters may have thought of the brush

to wit I am as free-spirited as any Roman

thinking about the surface as it reflects the depths

but history is the last thing poems should tell

and stories next to last so poetry is all

a scent of berry like a splash of destiny

which hints at the best of life and after its small

thrill passes like a small lost civilization

it can be solace and sadness as well

no matter how long I write how ill or well

the story say of a lost civilization

or that we might be last of the generations

the poem restores nothing

blueberries limes peaches my love zero

why then is the poet

the last to see as a god

that earth from the heavens is radiant fruit

CHERRIES BLUEBERRIES WHITE PEACHES AND LIMES

Glimpse

Eamon Grennan

Every so often, in the appalling state of the state he's in, he comes up for air
And finds his own death like a dog sleeping on wooden steps, which may wake
And bark if he makes the slightest sound. And when he glimpses that couple
Getting into their car together as they've been doing for years—the woman
Directing the man how to back out into traffic—then the map he's peering at
Grows cloud-covered, the names get blotted out, and the roads are only thin
Rivers of blood, winding nowhere. But, buried in the dust of too much, who
Will hear the man cry out, saying this is how the story puts an end to itself?
For every corner he's brought to a kind of order, another one lends itself
To a chaos of odd socks, middens of books, trunkfuls of outworn clothes. But
Somewhere in the heart's heaving, at its tangle-toil of rage, in the wasp-nest
Of his nervous system, a small scream is gathering strength, getting ready.

Transition: Inheriting Maps

Peg Boyers

Remember the maps, Father,
the ones we rescued
from the great purge
of papers and books
that day we moved you?
Maps from around the world,
souvenirs of our shared past.

Together at the filing cabinet—
you on the stool, I bending over you—
both of us straining to see without glasses,
measuring memory against grid,
matching history with place,
locating the whereness and whatness
of the intransitive *was*—
without object or home,

united in the grammar of common
longing, reaching back, together,
for clarity, pattern, design.
See how the angles and distance
define the faultlines,
account for time
—as if life could be surveyed
with tripod and transit.

OPEN CITY

The years reveal themselves in maps:
Port Harcourt, Pakanbaru,
Tripoli—petroleum cities by now
obliterated—unfold their spectral
streets to us, provide transitory homes
for the careless American diaspora.
Oil under it all.

Imperial, enchanted childhood!

Crude spurts up through the page,
staining present, blurring past,
the tanker at the dock
now in relief, your pipeline
unloaded, stretched out
across island, desert, harbor.

The box of maps spills
over with postcards and travel
brochures, snapshots of
Assam the gardener grinning
his fan-tooth smile,
Sunday and Uden and Marta,
in paper white uniforms, serving,
always serving brats and bosses
on three continents
forever.

The veined paper stretches
out between us, its red
and blue pulsing with codes
we both would decipher,
longitude and latitude obscurely
circumscribing the real:

Your freckled arm reaches for mine,
the mottled skin my legend,
bent arthritic finger my future.
My still strong hand
receives the maps,
appropriates the legacy,

folds the moment for later perusal
as you prepare for the next transfer.

"Galina turned onto her side. The whistling sounds that her daughter made drove her crazy, like the buzzing of a bunch of mosquitoes. So did Sergey's bursts of snoring. He lay on his back now. His mouth was agape. He reeked of onions and vodka. Galina buried her head under a pillow and sobbed." (Vapnyar, page 243)

This Man Is Eating in His Sleep

Jessica Lamb-Shapiro

THERE WAS A STORY ON THE NEWS ABOUT A WOMAN WHO drowned her kids and blamed it on the Indians, but where we lived there weren't any so she got picked up pretty quick. Her husband was flexing his teeth all over the papers, saying he understood she was under a lot of stress, the kids were rowdy and loud, the Indians were known drinkers and gamblers. He didn't seem to get it, and it was making me sad. He was talking on and on about forgiveness, and how no one could hurt him, he had so much love in his heart. He said the day after the drowning someone had stolen his car, and he didn't care. I thought about finding him and telling him his wife was a bitch, offering to make love to him, get married, whatever; he was good looking. I had seen his smiling face in the paper when I stopped to get gas. The thing that got me, in all the pictures he was wearing a diamond-patterned sweater vest. It reminded me of something that high school teachers wear when talking about *Beowulf*, and other primordial stuff.

I'd been driving behind an old brown car for a hundred miles. The vanity license plate read GARY. Every few minutes Gary would point theatrically at a car he passed, stretching his arm up and over the roof toward our right. His arm was thin and muscular, and had a tattoo I couldn't make out, or maybe a scar. I'd look at the people he'd indicated when I drove past. An exceptionally old man with damaged skin was picking things out of his mustache. I laughed; it was intensely gross. We played this game for some time. Once he pointed at nothing, and I realized he was telling me to pull over.

"Are you going to choke me?" I said, sticking out my arm with awkward formality.

"Do you want me to?" he replied.

I didn't know what to say. I felt tired and crazy; I hadn't eaten since morning. He was wearing a diamond-patterned sweater vest, like the guy from the news. I thought I was hallucinating; he didn't seem the type.

"You shouldn't pull off into the woods with strangers," said Gary.

In principal I agreed, but we were hardly twenty feet from the road. If he did try to choke me it would be in plain view of families; though, on the other hand, I'd be dead before they could pull off and reverse. We were near a colossal sign which read PRISON INMATES WORKING. I didn't see any, and I wondered if they just meant in general, somewhere.

"Want an ice cream?" he asked, thumbing in the direction of his trunk.

I nodded. The question made me feel instantly at ease. He opened a huge cooler filled with beers and made a big show of sifting through the ice. There were a bunch of clothes in the trunk, a car seat in the back.

"Kids?" I asked.

"Sure," he said, as though he'd heard of them. "Sorry," he said, handing me a beer. It was unbearably cold to touch.

"No ice cream?" I said.

"We take what we can get," he said magisterially. The statement annoyed me; I liked to believe I was holding out for something better. His face was bony and hard, his skin thinly stretched, like the headmaker had been stingy with the plushy matter that stuffs up the skull. We drank in silence for a while.

"That lady with the bird," he said suddenly.

I said, "Yikes."

A woman had been driving with a bird on her lap. Attached to her van was a covered wheel that had JUNE AND ED printed on it. I wondered if Ed was the bird. She was giving the bird little kisses, and the bird was pecking at her face, though not in a way that looked affectionate. Her face had fresh scars on it.

I hoped it wouldn't come to that for me, but at this point it wasn't looking too promising; I'd been thinking of getting a cat. I liked the idea of something small and furry that might want to lick me, but what if it died? What are you supposed to do with a cat if it dies? Dig a miniature grave? I wasn't very strong and I didn't own a shovel. I made a mental note to pick one up or get an axe. The beer was freezing my hand, so I switched it to the other fist.

"Weird," said Gary.

"Yeah," I said.

We looked at an empty house on a trailer bed that was drifting by, bumping obscenely. Something so big was unsuited for rapid movement; every other car was passing it. The trailer stretched the limits of the lane, threatening to usurp more than its fair share of the road; it gave me the same disquieted feeling I had when I would pull on a pair of jeans and find a sock stuck inside the leg.

"Boyfriend?" Gary asked.

"No," I said.

I had been seeing this guy Andy for a few months, except we hardly ever saw each other. He'd been recently married and his wife was a superlative bitch—they'd built several new wings onto their house before he figured out she was sleeping with the carpenter—so he wasn't all that psyched about women in general. I tried to explain that we weren't all hooked up to the same complex system of tubes, but he'd often point out ways that I was like her: the way I held my mouth, the books I liked, the sharp sudden breaths I took in sleep. Once when I was over at his place I asked him why he wanted to date me; he thought about it for a minute, then said, "I'm an asshole." Then he went into a small corner of the room and fiddled with something for about an hour. He was separating and regrouping a bunch of wires. His back was to me but every once in a while he let out a sound like he was choking. I guess he was suffering or something but it wasn't my fault; I was trying to be decent.

Gary smiled and some beer fell out of his mouth.

I said, "You?"

"Ha," he said. What kind of answer was that? I shifted uncomfortably.

"I've never done this sort of thing," I said.

"What sort of thing?"

I didn't know what to call it because I didn't know what it was. "You know," I said, gesturing abstractly.

"I know?" he smiled, something mean.

"Not that I'm always a good person or anything," I said in my defense.

"You're obviously a serious badass."

"I've done bad things," I said, trying to remember one of them.

"What's the worst thing you've ever done?" he asked, looking attentively at his shoe. There was something wrong about the way he'd tied his laces.

"Do you have a brother?" I asked.

He continued his examination of the shoe.

"I have a brother," I said. "He looks a lot like me. When I was a kid I'd dress up as a boy and we'd pass for twins."

This was true, except my brother was dead. The worst thing I'd ever done was to dress up like him at the funeral. I thought it would make everyone feel better, but instead they looked at me like I was a ghost. With my hair cut off even I didn't recognize myself in the mirror. I had smiled at my mother in a way that I thought was reassuring, but she started crying really hard. I felt bad about upsetting her. After that my parents were always quiet when I entered a room.

"Huh," he said, staring at nothing. I was getting nervous. It was hard for me to talk to people, and I felt like I was disappointing him.

"Do you want to make out?" I said. This was good: I knew I wasn't supposed to kiss strangers. I leaned against the car, remembering to smile. He twisted his torso in my direction and bent his legs, lifting me on to the trunk in a gesture that was, I thought, suspiciously smooth.

Gary put his mouth on top of mine. People could see us, but I hardly cared. In the past year I'd become one of those women who wore blouses instead of shirts, and earrings that didn't pass the lobe; I didn't care for this vision of myself. I looked up. The clouds were making shapes so big I couldn't see what they were, covering the last cords of sun. Birds circled the car; hawks, maybe. I was pleased with myself. I had seen something like this in a movie once, where the woman was beautiful and serene. The scene was really similar, I remembered, only I couldn't recall how it had ended.

I sat up and Gary stepped back, wiping his hands on his pants. He gave me an expectant look. I hunched toward him, but miscalculated the angle and fell past him off the trunk. I hit the back of my head on the bumper and the rough ground tore into my back.

"Am I bleeding?" I shouted. The question came out louder than I'd intended. I hated to bleed, and this turn of events was making me look distinctly less attractive.

"Yeah," he said, seeming impressed. I was getting blood on his car. It was smeared so lightly it looked like an inconsistency in the paint. I tried to rub at it with my finger but I only expanded the stain. Meanwhile, the birds were making a bloodsucking noise, and we didn't have any water to clean the wound.

"I'll pour some beer on it," he said. This struck me as very innovative if potentially unsanitary. The cut fizzed in a way which was more titillating than painful. I was having trouble with discrete shapes. I felt so tired. I wanted to put my head down on the concrete. I closed my eyes and let the gravel press into my cheek.

"Do you know about spiders?" he said.

"I know they're gross and hairy," I muttered. I could barely stay awake.

"I saw a television program this morning on spiders, how they procreate. The male chases the female around a tree branch. It's funny because they look the same. Then he uses his legs to hold her in place and avoid her fangs. There's some poking signal for her to raise her abdomen, though I'm not really sure where that is in all the hair and legs and eyes. Then the male inserts his claw, that's what they called it, into her midsection. Insemination can last for hours or seconds; then the male has to split or she'll eat him."

It occurred to me that this was a creepy tangent for him to take.

"Go then," I said, falling asleep.

The birds made a shushing noise with their wings.

But when I woke up he was still there. I wondered how much time had passed. My back hurt worse and I had dirt in my mouth. He was asleep next to me, his mouth gnawing silently on air. I shifted and he jumped up.

"I thought you were dead." He scratched at his face.

"No such luck," I said.

He didn't respond. He stared at my forehead. I was starting to feel like he had seen too much of my disgrace in too short a time. I crossed my arms and tried to look nonchalant.

"Do you know that you were chewing in your sleep?" I said. He made wrinkles in his face so that it looked very serious.

"I usually dream about eating. Once I even woke up on the floor by the refrigerator, surrounded by food."

I laughed at the idea: Gary sitting in eggs and bacon, chocolate cake, cold lasagna, the plastic door wide open, the interior light shining reproachfully in his eyes. He frowned at my levity. I felt suddenly guilty, and tried to make it up to him.

"Do you want to keep making out?" I said.

"Not really."

"Because I'm bloody and dirty?"

"No." But I was sure he was lying.

"We take what we can get!" I said, hoping it didn't sound too desperate.

He said, "I do."

I didn't like the way he was smiling. I put my hand behind his neck, but he waved it away.

"Don't you like women?"

"Why do you say that?"

"I think you hate women," I said. I picked up a handful of dirt and small rocks and threw it toward the woods, then wiped my hand on the edge of his car.

"Don't be a bitch," he said quietly. A police car drove by.

"What's the worst thing you've ever done?" I asked.

His face shifted as though it were resetting. "Get in the car."

The police car had pulled off and was reversing in our direction. It was dark out, and I couldn't see the birds, but I figured they were still lurking; I was happy to move into the car. The policeman walked over in a half-successful imitation of a slow cowboy. He and Gary talked for several minutes, but I couldn't hear what they were saying. Gary waved his arms wildly about as though he were defending himself against a large bear; the policeman nodded with quiet sympathy. The policeman knocked sharply on my window. I rolled it down with deliberate gravity, like I had seen actors do when playing criminals.

"Everything okay, Ma'am?" he asked, with an accent that seemed affected. I wondered how Gary had accounted for my bloody clothes. Gary was smiling and chewing on his lip. I thrust a hysterical finger in his direction.

"This man is eating in his sleep!" I said.

Gary and the policeman exchanged a knowing glance. He asked to see my license and looked half-heartedly for something in my purse, maybe weapons and drugs. Not finding any, he frowned, shook hands with Gary, and slowly swaggered away. Gary hopped in the driver's seat.

"Are you looking to go to jail, Miss?" he said.

"No."

"Why would you do such a stupid thing?"

This was agitating; I made a huffing noise. Gary was unmoved. I didn't get it: nothing seemed to bother this man. I took off my shirt and flung it in the backseat. The air vents were blowing and it made my breasts feel cold and shriveled. I said, "What's the worst thing you've ever done?"

"Jesus," he said. He took out his wallet and returned it to his pocket. He put his hands on the steering wheel, feeling it slowly all over, then gripping it fiercely like he was trying to hold it in place. I put my hands in my armpits for warmth. I started to speak, but he grabbed my face and turned it toward the car window. He flipped on the harsh interior light. My reflection was a distorted curve.

"Do you think you're pretty?"

"Sure," I said. I didn't know the right answer to that one. His hand was on the back of my head.

"What do you have to offer the world?"

"Breasts?"

He closed his fingers tightly on my hair. I instantly regretted the joke; there was something serious in the rigidity of his arms. He pulled out a sharp metal object from his back pocket. I'd seen it before; it was some sort of instrument used for cutting ceramic tiles in bathrooms. It was black and had an arrow-shaped head. Andy had one that had belonged to the carpenter; it was the only thing he'd saved from his marriage. I guess he'd kept it to remind himself to be wry and sadly ironic all of the time.

"Do you think anybody wants you?"

"Sure," I said. "Why not?" There were a lot of people alive, though I knew I wouldn't meet them all.

"Do you think anybody wants you?"

Something huge rushed by on the road, another house. For a second, I imagined I saw people in there, a man and a woman; they were smiling and making breakfast. He was cooking while she gently placed forks on a table. I thought of my grandmother, how she let me have hot melted chocolate for breakfast. She'd lived in the same house since she was born.

He placed the tool on his leg. I didn't say anything. I noticed his eyes were closed. How long had they been like that?

"I'm lonely, too," he said.

"I'm not lonely," I said.

"Don't lie to me."

"I'm not lying," I said. "You're being terrible."

"I know when I'm being terrible."

"You're evil." The words sounded familiar, like maybe they were part of a line from that movie. I was still trying to remember what had happened. There was something valuable he had that the actress had wanted, like a gold ring, that had belonged to her good-hearted, mustachioed father.

"You want to see something evil?" he asked. I didn't.

He pulled out his wallet. There were a few dollars and a picture of some kids in it. They looked familiar.

"Are those your kids?"

"Ha," he said.

"Are they?" I asked him.

"It's not my car," he said. "That's the truth."

I had seen the kids before, in the paper. This was the same picture they had printed. The kids belonged to the man with the vest. His name was Gary.

"You stole the car?"

"There were twenty of these vests in the trunk," he said in disbelief. My arms felt gelatinous. I wanted to cry.

"Do you want one?" he asked.

"No."

I thought about the man and his dead children: nothing scared him; nothing made him sad. If I could find him, he could teach me to have love in my heart.

"Gary," I started.

"Don't call me that," he said.

This man, not Gary, was softly touching the picture. "I want some of these," he said. There were two girls and a boy. They had fat cheeks, and they were looking at something to the left of the camera.

"Those kids are dead."

"I didn't kill them."

"What's your name?"

His hand traced the pattern on his chest in small precise undulations. "I like this vest because of the diamonds, how they overlap."

"I like it, too." There was something reassuring about the vest.

"Exactly." He paused. "It's what you want."

I didn't say anything. He covered my hand and squeezed it, too hard. I jerked away. "Don't be afraid."

"I'm not afraid."

"Do you know what I'm talking about?"

"Sure," I said.

"You're not listening to me."

I said I was. I asked him if he knew the movie I was thinking about; he did. I asked him if he remembered how it ended.

"They were both decapitated."

"I would have remembered that," I said. I looked crossly at the window, though I couldn't see a thing outside.

He put his hand on my neck.

"Do you think anybody wants you?"

"It's late," I said. I took the keys from my purse.

"Do you?"

"What?" I placed my hand on the door.

"Do you think anybody wants you?" He was biting hard on the corner of his lip, and it made his mouth look stepped on.

"Yes. OK." I reached for the handle.

"Do you think anybody wants you?"

"Yes," I said. I pulled the handle, but he clamped his hand over the lock.

"Don't you ever tell the truth?"

It's freezing outside, so you don't mind that downtown is now a giant tangled mess of careless architecture, though you are aware that this sort of over-the-top retail has stripped Indianapolis of any individuality it may have once possessed. You recall it having individuality, but you can't be sure. (Poirier, page 39)

Devil Milk

Stu Mead

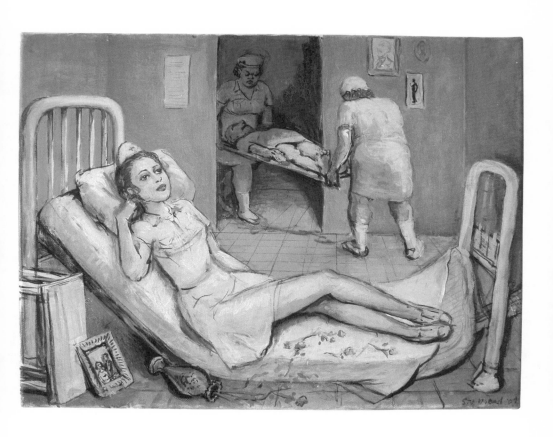

The Life and Times of a Forty-Nine Pound Man

Rick DeMarinis

NICK PITMAN ASKED HIS FATHER TO COME TO WEST TEXAS FOR A visit. Nick's wife, Vasilisa Ivanovna Petrovich, believed the visit would turn out badly. "Big motherfucking mistake," she said. "Bruno thinks you are failure. You know what is to happen, don't you?"

Nick had exposed her to the choice American expletives and Vasilisa used them with reckless abandon, believing it enhanced her fluency. She was right about Bruno, but Nick hoped that the old man would come to see that his only son hadn't made such a mess of his life after all. Nick taught English composition to techie-wannabees at Western States Institute of Mining and Metallurgy. The English department was small and neglected by the college administration whose priorities were the engineering and business schools, but Nick was content in spite of the secret life he had to live.

His secret life was his science fiction career, which had just reached a kind of apogee: Cockatrice Special Effects, Inc. had taken an option to make a feature film of his new novel, *The Life and Times of a Forty-Nine Pound Man.* His department chairman regarded science fiction as an unworthy genre, a spurious form completely at odds with the higher goals of literature.

Nick was aware of the higher goals of literature, and hoped someday to write a novel that could sit comfortably on the same shelf with the work of Bradbury and Heinlein, perhaps even with the genre-transcending works of Vonnegut and Orwell. But if he wanted tenure—and he wanted it badly—he'd have to keep his science fiction career to himself. His job kept food on the table, paid the rent, and supported his writing. It was a safety net he could not do without.

His father had no respect for teaching as a career for men. He thought teaching was an occupation originally intended for women. Men who chose to teach over jobs in the competitive workplace were either loafers, incompetents, misfits, or homosexuals. A career in writing, unless it turned out to be lucrative, was even less defensible. And writers who wrote for writing's sake, who lived in willful poverty, were in the same category as street people. Bruno Pitman believed the only reliable indicator of success was the size of a man's bank account and the credit limit of his platinum card.

"Worthless is as worthless does," he was fond of saying.

But at least Nick could show the old man a Xerox of the ten-thousand dollar check he had received from Cockatrice. If his work meant nothing to his father, maybe the evidence of serious cash would.

Bruno Pitman was a retired bank president who now lived in the Bahamas with his fourth wife, Winona Mufkey, a twenty-three-year-old model. At seventy-four he still bristled with aggressive good health and offensive opinions. He was a big man, over six feet tall, with a great round stomach that pushed out in front of him like blunt warning: move out of the way or get dumped on your keester. He had a big hairless dome pink with blood pressure, a jaw strong enough to carry leaflard jowls, a nose as thick and as red as a peeled yam. His black unforgiving eyes were as hard and as expressionless as nail-heads. He reminded Nick of old photographs of J. P. Morgan, the railroad baron.

"I'm here for five hours, then I fly back to Nassau," he said when Nick picked him up at the airport. "Where's your chubby little red-haired Rooskie?"

"Vasi went ahead to the Weston, to get us a table," Nick said, hoping his father wouldn't refer to Vasilisa's weight problem at the restaurant. Vasilisa was an unashamed eater. She'd nearly starved to death in Russia years ago, and Nick did not begrudge her occasional self-indulgence. "They wouldn't give us reservations because they've got a union convention this weekend."

"Unions," his father muttered as he lit a cigar. "Blackmailers and extortionists. Featherbedding in the name of social progress. You two got a little Pitman on the way yet, Nick?"

"We'll probably adopt, Dad."

Bruno Pitman narrowed his eyes suspiciously. *"Adopt?* What the hell do you want to do that for? Have your own, like your sister down in Coral Gables. She's got, what—four babies now. She's given me my only grandkids." Bruno Pitman had a proud gleam in his hard little eyes, as if he had sired the four babies himself.

"We can't have kids, Dad. I'm sterile."

"You're *what?* Oh for Chrissakes, you mean you can't . . . ? Bruno's pink dome paled. "Jesus, Nick, they've got this drug now. It's called Viagra. I use it myself."

"I'm not impotent, Dad. Just a disastrously low sperm count. Down in the low millions per milliliter of semen—something like that."

"Sterile, impotent, what's the difference? Bottom line is you can't make babies. It's your mother's fault. I should never have married her. She drank when she was pregnant with you. That's why you've got bandy legs and why your eyes are so far apart. It's probably why you can't get a decent job. Fetal alcohol syndrome. Remember how all the neighbor kids use to call you Geeko? Your mother was an airline stewardess when I met her. Breathed too much rarefied air on top of those mickey-sized bottles of Jamaican rum. She came into our marriage with damaged chromosomes. She should have had a warning label pinned on her."

Nick let his father rave on without protest. He was used to this.

Dinner was just as Vasilisa predicted: A nonstop monologue by Bruno that analyzed, mocked, and denounced. His targets were mainly lefty politicians, but he also took on the media—newspapers, television, Hollywood. He gradually lowered his sights until they came to rest, finally, on Nick.

"So tell me, son," he said. "When are you going to buy yourself some decent clothes and get a real job? You can't expect to spend the rest of your life living from hand to mouth on teacher's pay."

Nick took the opportunity to fish out the Xeroxed check from Cockatrice. "I think my writing career is about to take off, Dad," he said. "This is just for a six-month option. When they make the film, they'll pay me two percent of production costs. That could be well up into six figures, maybe seven."

Bruno Pitman was not impressed. "When, when, when," he said. "That's one of the most pathetic words in the English language, along with 'maybe,' 'if,' 'might,' and 'could be.'"

Vasilisa buttered her third dinner roll, looked at it, decided to leave it on her plate. She leaned toward Nick. "Tell old shit-eater to motherfuck himself," she whispered into his ear.

"You shouldn't eat so much starch, Vasi," Bruno said. "It goes straight to your hips. I don't let Winona eat wheat or potato products at all. I limit her diet to fruits, fresh green vegetables and lamb chops."

"We must take you back to airport, Papa," Vasilisa hissed, her lips compressed to a thin red line.

Hans Ludens, president of Cockatrice, called Nick at home. He wanted Nick to come to Los Angeles to talk about the script. "This is going to be the first major sci-fi film of the twenty-first century," he said. "I want your script to be hotter than *Bladerunner*. I want to make Kubrick's *2001* look like it was made by Ed Wood. You with me on this, Nick?"

"Script?" he said. "I didn't know you wanted me to do a script."

"Who else if not you? It's *your* book. You da *man,* Nick. Don't worry, you'll get help."

Nick kissed Vasilisa goodbye at the airport. "You be good," she said.

"I'd rather be lucky than good," he said, quoting Lefty Gomez, the Yankee southpaw from the 1930s. It was one of his favorite expressions.

"You speak of movie, yes?" she said, raising an eyebrow.

"Honey, that's the only thing on my mind, believe me," he said.

Rodney McQuirk, a cameraman at Cockatrice, picked Nick up at LAX. McQuirk, a lanky, sullen man whose breath was laced with the dark fumes of cirrhosis, said, "Good novel, dude. I'm the one who recommended it to Hans. Looks like we might even shoot the mother, if the money people come across with a real budget."

The Cockatrice studio was located in Van Nuys. Rodney drove an ancient Volvo coupe with no muffler. Conversation during the long ride to Van Nuys was impossible over the sputtering roar. Nick occupied himself by trying to visualize the storyboards for the script he would write.

The Life and Times of a Forty-Nine Pound Man was about a retirement community on Mars. Mars was ideal for old-age homes because gravity on the red planet was one-third that of earth's. The senior citizens would live under a Sundome, a huge canopy a hundred times bigger than the canopies covering the largest malls on earth. This would be structurally possible because of the low gravity. The steel used for the dome's construction would come from the iron ore mined on Mars. There would be giant lenses built into the canopy which would focus and concentrate sunlight, making the otherwise frigid climate of Mars as mild as south Florida in winter. The weak pull of gravity would also have all sorts of spin-off health benefits. Arthritis, for example, would be a far less painful affliction on Mars. The brittle bones of those suffering from osteoporosis would be less likely to break. The feeblest man or woman would be able to move furniture around their condos with relative ease. Little old ladies, palsied and vague and bent with widow's humps, would have strength comparable to an earthbound stevedore's. The aging process itself would slow down: a year on Mars lasts 687 earth days and time would thus be naturally dilated and slowed, which in turn would retard the deterioration of cells. The appearance of the senior citizens would even begin to change—they'd start growing again because of the lessened gravity. A man who had been five-foot-ten might discover suddenly that he is six-foot-three—a dramatic reversal of the geriatric "shrinkage" people suffer on Earth. And as the bodies of the seniors elongated, they'd also slim down. Even the sexual drive would enjoy a renaissance, and the coital positions made possible by the weak pull of gravity would astound the most jaded sex addict. A forty-nine pound roué would enjoy sexual gymnastics he could only dream about on earth.

Nick pictured the opening scene: the interplanetary shuttle, packed with seniors and their nurses, slipping into orbit around the red planet. He scripted some dialogue in his head:

FRETFUL OLD MAN
Are we there yet, Miss?

ATTRACTIVE YOUNG NURSE
You betcha, Mr. Ainsworthy!

You're just going to *love* Martian Meadows!

Hans Ludens was a big man dressed entirely in black leather. He sat on a motorcycle inside his office. The office looked like it belonged in a meat-packing plant. A bare bulb hung from the ceiling on its cord. The plank floor was worn and splintered. Luden's desk was gray steel. It was piled high with notebooks and unidentifiable pieces of hi-tech, low-tech, and retro-tech equipment. There were posters on the walls from movies Cockatrice had provided the special effects for: *Red Moon, Black Star, Water Planet, Stone Clone.* A papier mâché sculpture, female, wearing camouflage fatigues—clung to the exposed wall studs halfway to the ceiling. Her eyes were wide with adrenaline, and her mouth was open in an exultant cry, the paper teeth white as Chiclets. The sculpture was titled: "Fearless Climber."

"Nick, you're still alive!" Ludens boomed. "That car of El Rodney's is a death trap. I would've sent Lana Faye or Bobbi Jo in the Mercedes, but El Rodney here is your biggest fan. He wanted the honor."

Ludens kick-started the motorcycle—a vintage Harley Electraglide. He twisted the throttle, filling the room with thunder and blue haze, then shut the machine down. He stepped off and shook Nick's hand in a crushing grip. "We're going to make the bitchinest movie out of your bitchin book, have no fear."

Nick knew he was supposed to be impressed. And he was. So here was life in the fast lane! What a fine romantic world Hans Luden lived in, a world where you could wear black leather and call people "El Rodney" and not feel foolish. It was like an extension of childhood, permitting yourself to dress in costume and play out any game that came to mind. What a great stay against the death grips of responsibility, good behavior, and age.

They toured the studio—"my factory," Ludens called it—before they went to lunch. The tour didn't mean much to Nick—he was technically illiterate. Hans, taking note of Nick's bewilderment, said, "Once you've seen one laser you've seen them all, right?" Now and then Hans would relight his cigar and blow smoke into a ruby red laser beam. He'd study the patterns the smoke made for minutes before moving on to the next machine. Computer-controlled cameras on rails were positioned in front of models of space vehicles, from orbital space stations to interstellar transport ships. Rodney, the cameraman, showed Nick how these cameras worked, how models were photographed against a blue screen, and Nick pretended to grasp the details.

Hans decided lunch would be out on Catalina Island. They drove to Newport Beach in Luden's Mercedes convertible. Ludens steered with one hand as he weaved in and out of traffic at ninety miles per hour. A woman—Bobbi Jo—sat next to Ludens. She was a blonde with spiked hair and nose rings. Her ears looked like a metal recycling depot. She had a sultry, challenging look that she was evidently unable to turn off. She regarded everything, from her black-glossed fingernails to Nick's elbow-patched sports coat, with the same smoldering hostility. In spite of her demeanor and appearance, she was friendly enough, and spoke in the honeysuckle accents of a 1950ish southern belle.

Nick rode in the backseat with Lana Faye Harmon, a twenty-year-old actress with long black hair that billowed and furled in the eddying wind like thick smoke. She seemed more sophisticated than her years. Nick thought that women like Lana Faye were born sophisticated. He felt over his head just sitting next to her.

At Newport Beach they boarded a seaplane, a converted World War II PBY sub-chaser. Hans put on an old army air corps cap with a "thirty-mission crush," swiped, he said, from the set of *The Memphis Belle.* The plane belonged to Cockatrice, Inc. The image of a Cockatrice—the mythical snake hatched from a cock's egg—had been painted on the hull of the flying boat. The snake's silver-green scales were big as shingles. The pink mouth with its yellow fangs yawned under the pilot's cabin. The lethal red eyes of the cockatrice stared malevolently.

It made Nick nervous to board an airplane that had as its insignia an image of unrepentant evil. It seemed to mock any benevolent forces the universe might be harboring. Flight always made Nick nervous under the best auspices. He seldom flew anywhere, but when he did he'd revert to his grade school Catholicism and recite the Rosary under his breath until the plane was safely in the stratosphere, flying level. Then he'd repeat the ritual as the plane descended.

Nick sat in one of the huge Plexiglas observation blisters built into the side of the hull. A small sofa had been custom-fitted into this area. Lana Faye curled up next to him. Ludens flew the plane and Bobbi Jo sat in the copilot's seat. Ludens started the engines, revved them, and the flying boat began to plow out of its harbor and into the open bay.

They flew low over the gentle green swells. Schools of flying fish broke through the glossy surface as if showing off for the PBY.

Lana Faye scooted close to Nick. "Writers fascinate me," she said. "I mean, how do you come up with all this stuff?" she said.

"I don't know," Nick said. "It just comes to me, like it's in the air."

"You mean like a flu bug. You sort of catch it?"

"Yeah, like that," Nick said. "It's a kind of chronic disease. Incurable." *Dad would agree,* Nick thought.

A sudden turbulence made Lana Faye roll against Nick. When the air smoothed, she didn't move away. "You're a cute guy, Nick, in a goofy sort of way. You ever mess around?" she asked.

"I'm married," Nick said.

"And your point is?" Lana Faye said.

His mouth went dry. The Plexiglas turret filled with blinding sunlight as the plane leaned into a lazy turn. Nick felt a twinge of disappointment with himself. Here he was, flying over the Pacific in a converted sub-chaser with a beautiful young woman next to him, a movie deal in the works, and all he could do was offer lame excuses. He was not a romantic adventurer like his father. Bruno Pitman demeaned Nick not only because he was an underpaid teacher, but because he had no sense of adventure. Nick was a mild-mannered observer of life, not a reckless participant.

He preferred it that way. He thought his reasons were good. He led a careful and structured existence because he was aware how delicate the thread was that held things together. You did not risk the things you valued most. It suited him. But it was not the worldview of a Hollywood player.

"I love my wife," he said, shrugging. "She's Russian," he added.

"Well good for you and good for her," Lana Faye said, yawning. Her mouth was pink with animal health. "I respect that in a man. You're a quality guy, Nick. I mean that." She lit a cigarette.

"Actually she's Estonian," he said. "Her name is Vasilisa. Her father was shot by the Communists and her grandfather was shot by the Nazis and her great-grandfather was exiled to Siberia by the Romanovs."

"She's got rebel blood," Lana Faye said. "She a wild one, Nick? You able to keep her happy?" She gave Nick a sly sidelong grin.

"She escaped the Iron Curtain with her mother and two sisters," Nick said. "They rode hundreds of miles in an unheated boxcar in the middle of winter from Tartu to Riga to Kaunas. They nearly starved to death. Then they hid on a boat that was headed for Sweden. Her little sister died on the way."

"Heavy," Lana Faye said, blowing a cloud of blue smoke into the lasering sun.

"I'm loyal as a spaniel," he said. "If anyone deserves loyalty, it's Vasi."

"Stay cool, Nick. I'm not going to pull your chubby out of your Dockers. I'm with someone anyway. An actor. His agent calls him the next Brad Pitt."

"The *next* Brad Pitt?"

"They come and they go, Nick. Everyone's a temp."

Bobbi Jo staggered toward them, her hands gripping the exposed ribs of the fuselage struts. "He wants you up front," she said.

Nick poked himself in the chest. "Me?"

"You. He needs you."

Nick crawled past Bobbi Jo and into the front cabin of the PBY. Crash dummies dressed in flight suits and wearing old Army Air Corps sheepskin caps were seated at the radio operator's console and at the navigator's desk.

"Hey, Nick," Ludens said. "Sit down."

Nick sat in the copilot's seat.

"You want to fly this crate for a while? I'm going back to take a piss."

"I'm not a pilot, Hans."

"No sweat. We're flying by wire. You got the wheel, but you won't have to horse it around. No primitive hydraulic servo mechanisms to do your bidding. You fuck up, cause a pilot-induced oscillation, the computer will put the damper on it. I paid a cool five mil to upgrade the old Cockatrice. Go on, Ace, take the fucking yoke."

Ludens pointed at an instrument. "That's a level-flight indicator. All you got to do is keep the nose on the horizon and that bubble on the line. The horizon moves up into your view, you know your descending. If you're in doubt, check the bubble. Take your cue from the engines, they'll talk to you." Ludens lit a cigar. "Keep us out of the drink, Nick. The only tough thing about a flying boat is putting her down in chop."

"Chop?" Nick asked, as if that was the only part of Luden's mono-logue he did not understand.

"Gnarly water. Like putting down in a potato patch."

He was thrilled. He felt adventure in the tingling vibrations the engines produced in the yoke. The tingle traveled up his arms and across his chest and back to his spine. He felt it in his crotch. It gave him a partial erection. He pushed the yoke forward and leveled off a hundred feet above the ocean's glossy swells. A school of flying fish rose out of the water off the starboard wing like aquatic angels. Every creature on earth loved to play. Why not Nick Pitman?

He eased the yoke back and started a slow climb into the afternoon sun. The ocean became smooth as oil cloth, a silver arm of sunlight bisecting it all the way to the western horizon. Nick listened to the heavy throb of the lugging engines, watched the altimeter tick off the increasing altitude. His ears popped.

At nine thousand feet he pushed the yoke forward. He felt himself rise off the seat, his thighs straining against the lap belt. He felt the insignificant weight of his presence on the planet. He sensed the canard gravity had imposed on the world: Gravity was the mother and father of all restraint, even the self-imposed kind. The world was heavy and the things of the world had real weight.

Weight was the key: you had weighty thoughts, you made weighty decisions, you weighed carefully your every move, and there were so many things that weighed on your mind. What was the soundbite that had surfaced during the recent national elections? *Gravitas.* A man without gravitas was not fit to shoulder the weight of leadership. Nick wanted no part of gravitas. He wanted to be lighthearted, unburdened, a blithe spirit skimming weightlessly through the vast and intricate world, knowing there was nothing to lose. Was it possible? Had it ever been possible?

When the Cockatrice reached the top of the parabolic arc before it began its shallow dive, Nick started laughing hysterically. Truth hit him like a pie in the face. He thought: *The forty-nine pound man, c'est moi!* His novel, ostensibly science fiction, was really about him, about his longing to free himself of all artificial restraint. He was not even forty years old, but he could see how the rest of his life would go. No adventures, no surprises, but plenty of dependable security—tenure, generous annuities provided by his college, and then social security and medicare. Nothing ever to worry about again, except that he was locking himself in a very narrow space, cozy as a coffin.

The horizon rose in the windshield and disappeared above it. The engines raced. They howled like twin banshees. Hans Ludens stumbled into the cabin. "What the hell are you doing to my airplane, Nick?" he said. "You made me piss all over myself! The girls are terrified! Ease back on the yoke, cowboy, you're going to tear the wings off my bird!" Ludens slid into the pilot's seat and took over the controls. He flew the PBY the rest of the way to Catalina and put it down in the smooth waters of Avalon Bay.

They hiked up the hill above the bay to an Andalusian restaurant. They sat in a narrow booth and ordered margaritas and paella. Nick had three margaritas before the paella came. At one point, Lana Faye put her hand on Nick's thigh and squeezed. "I think you're some kind of crazy man," she said, her breath sultry and close. "Are you some type of intellectual adrenaline freak, Nick?"

"The Texas cowboy's a stone cold troublemaker," Hans Ludens said, winking, and they all saluted Nick with their margaritas.

Nick never made trouble for anyone. He avoided trouble. Now he saw that trouble was a way to break out of the box. Without trouble you stayed safe in your homemade prison. Where you eventually shriveled. He felt drunk with this idea, which was both frightening and exhilarating. "Temps," he said. "We're temps, all of us."

He left the table and found a telephone booth and called Vasilisa.

"Vasi, I'm quitting my job," he said. "We're moving to L.A."

Nick misinterpreted the silence on the other end of the line. "It'll be okay, honey," he said. "We'll be fine. I'm going to make it. And you know what? It won't matter if I don't."

"Nicky," Vasilisa said. "Sit down, take deep breath. Your papa, he has passed."

It seemed like a rebuttal rather than bad news. It didn't fully register. "Vasi, listen to me. I'm through playing it safe." Then it hit him. "Passed? You mean Bruno is *dead*?"

"I am so sorry, my dear. It was motherfucking heart attack, this morning."

Vasilisa's use of the old-fashioned "my dear" touched him. His eyes welled up.

"Your papa, he took Viagra on top of nitroglycerin pills. Then fucked-up blood pressure dropped to zero. Poor little Mufkey, trapped under big dead body, feeling big dead body get cold."

Bruno dead? How could that be? He was a monument, a colossus.

"You are free, Nikita," Vasilisa said. She was crying, too. "No more you must kiss papa's big fat ass."

Nick brushed his tears away. He went back to the table and finished his fourth margarita. Bruno, the old risk-taker, dead. Died atop the bimbo. Nick smiled, thinking of the skinny model stuck under Bruno's cooling bulk, but it was not a cruel smile.

It wasn't the worst way to go. You could live to be a hundred, tied to tubes and respirators in the impersonal white walls of a nursing home on Mars, Martian nurses probing your almost non-existent forty-nine-pound body with their long clammy fingers, the sun in the glass ceiling thin as a dime.

Nick didn't love Bruno, he could admit that easily and without guilt, but he felt sorrow anyway. Sorrow was a prepackaged feature of the human psyche, one of the weights built into the genetic code.

Nick looked at the faces of the people around him. Strangers, strangers to him and to themselves. It didn't matter. They were all temps, but having a very good time anyway. He wouldn't mention Bruno. There would be no point in adding unnecessary weight to the splendid afternoon. He ordered another round of margaritas.

Dance with Me Ish, Like When You Was a Baby

Jesse Goldstein

MY BROTHER CALLS AND TELLS ME TO COME HOME. I DRIVE south along Highway 1 from Oregon, stopping for a nap on a bluff just outside Morro Bay. It is almost sunset and the tide is waning.

I get to my father's in the early morning. It is dark out and the key fumbles in my hands. I open the door to see my brother asleep in a chair beside him. My feet don't make a sound on the wood floor. The moonlight pours over my father's shoulder and I can see how his skin has cascaded on top of itself in layers of decay, cracked and dry, like a creek with no water. The house is stale with heat.

His body is crumpled and creased. I crouch down in front of him and tap my fingers on his knee cap; every six taps he chokes on his breath and snorts. I pat his forehead and comb his hair. Most has fallen but what is left is gray and matted.

"Ish," he says, opening his eyes. "Aren't you cold? It's so cold in here."

"No, I'm not cold Abs," I pull another blanket over him, tucking the ends beneath his toes.

"Did you see the ocean today? The surf is up. South swell. Wintertime," he says nodding his head.

"First Point not Third. I looked through the telescope, but I don't see so well. But you could see it in front, big waves, loud ones. Boom. Boom. How's that cold water in Lincoln City, kill you yet?"

"No, it ain't killed me Abs."

"Would've killed me."

He opens his eyes and they look like clouds.

"I got this pain in my chest, reminds me of when I used to peddle you around on the tandem. You just sat on the back and asked me to tell you stories. But I was working like a dog."

He motions his hand toward mine and I take it. It twitches cold in my palm. Sometimes rotting things are beautiful. The way forms break down, still showing life but in a manner of dying.

"Pick me up," he says. "I been waiting all evening to go for a walk."

I take his feet in my hand, delicately, the way I hold my newborn child, and place them in his slippers.

I layer him in blankets and lock my arms around his lower back, pulling him to his feet with my thighs. He tries to stand and wobbles forward into my chest, his arms branching over my body.

"Let's see, I can do this," he says shuffling left foot in front of right. "Twenty paces to the Westmoreland, twelve to the door." He exhales and braces his weight against my shoulder. He moves slow, our breaths counting out time in the dark room. "Maybe we can just go out on the deck," he says, breathing heavy, and I guide him the few steps outside, overlooking the ocean. He leans against the railing and I stand next to him.

We don't speak. My father has always been content staring at the sea and I stare as well. He breathes in deliberate gusts, moving in and out and the cold of his body makes him shiver. The tide laps on the sand, but I cannot hear it. I watch my father watch the ocean, and his eyes are tired sacks and it makes me sick. My stomach tightens. This will be done soon. The ocean is big, the tide is beckoned and pushed by the moon. Swells of saltwater are produced by wind thousands of miles away, and soon my father will be gone and his eyes will shrivel up and turn hard like rocks. Then I will share this with my son. I will get his feet wet and covered in sand.

"Ish," my father says, "you remember?" His eyes are already dead. "Please, my youngest son, you remember?"

And I do. When I was younger while visiting my grandfather in Florida, my father told me if he should ever turn down a walk along the boardwalk as my grandfather did, that I should set my mark and kill him right then.

"Please Ish, please, remember," he says.

My hands throw mad for his face, my fingers digging into his soft cheeks. I cover his mouth and plug his nose shut. He tries to speak but his words muffle in the creases of my hands and I press myself against him. We rest on the railing. It is silent but my body is pushing. Even my violent arms seem hushed in the night sky. His eyes are rolling back now and his skin is translucent with the moonlight on top of his forehead. And why do I have to do this? The flaky skin of his nostrils crack into my fingernails, and he is anxious, his skin sweats cold onto my chest, and my hands want to pull away and pet his hair, to grab his shoulders and shake him to life as if a shock will make him lively. He is going and I will stay.

His breathing slows, it no longer rests in the porous connections of my fingers, and I place my tips at the front of his lips and can feel his air seep out. So I thrust my hands again and smother him. I do not know how long it is until he is all done and gone, but I look at him and swear I can hear him say, "Dance with me Ish, like when you was a baby." And I tackle his dead body and fold his arm over my shoulder, and lead him through a two step, just like when I was younger and we danced the tango outside the house, watching the airplanes fly over the sea.

Alex
thought
of
that
old
joke
about
the
chicken
and
the
egg going to bed together. Afterward, the egg lights a cigarette. "Okay," she says to the chicken. "I guess that settles that." (Weiner, page 71)

sexy clowns
a project by sophie toulouse

november 12, 2002, east 3rd street, nyc

january 10, 2003, boulevard st. germain, paris

q: who am i?
a: i am a sexy clown

Physical Discipline

Greg Ames

IN THE WINTER OF 1983, WHEN I WAS TWELVE YEARS OLD, MY older sister Cathy carried a ventriloquist's dummy with her wherever she went. The dummy's name was Marilyn and at first nobody had the heart to tell Cathy that Marilyn was not really a dummy, but was in fact a charred strip of bark from our fireplace. But what could we do? Cathy skated freely on the frozen pond of her imagination, and as she wasn't hurting anybody but herself we generally ignored her eccentricities. She had just turned thirteen. Every night she slept with this burnt, splintered wood in her narrow bed, she snuggled with it on the sofa after school while she watched soap operas and sitcoms, and she left big black streaks across everything she touched, from the refrigerator door, to my previously white gerbils. Mr. Barker, Cathy's homeroom teacher, was concerned. The school psychologist, Nancy Palermo, asked my father if we had recently lost any family members to a house blaze or a fiery car crash. My father answered in the negative. Ms. Palermo wanted to see Cathy three times a week after school for private consultations.

We lived in a tiny, crumbling, yellow brick house on Hood Lane in Kenmore, New York, a suburb of Buffalo. All the houses on Hood Lane were the same size. Our street appealed to young couples just starting out, elderly folks in pajamas, recovering addicts trying to get a fresh start in life one day at a time, single women in their thirties who owned many cats, and struggling small business owners. There were no block parties or street games. But every now and then some drunk kid would crash his father's car into a tree and we'd all gather around, swimming in the headlights.

My mother's absence from our lives—she said she was "just getting her head straight" in Tampa St. Pete—forced my father to become the sole nurturer in our household, a terrible burden added to his already overwhelming duties as paragon and provider. He was a dry drunk. He hadn't touched a drink in over five years. But when my mother left for Florida, he stopped going to his meetings and stayed home with us.

"The other kids will make fun of you. You don't want that, do you, honey?" he said to Cathy. Unwrapping a lollipop, he paced in front of my sister, who was seated on the family room sofa clutching Marilyn to her breast like some horribly burned infant. I sat cross-legged on the floor at Pops' feet, paying close attention because I knew that someday I'd need to write all this down, just in case somebody asked me why I behave the way I do. "Ventriloquists are . . . annoying." He winced. "And nobody really likes them."

Arms crossed, Cathy brooded on the sofa. "That's not true," she murmured. "A lot of people like them."

"Sure, a few morons in the audience chuckle," he went on, "but only because they're embarrassed for the ridiculous sap who totes a stupid dummy around. Really. It's old hat. Fifties Vegas crap. That type of humor doesn't appeal to us anymore. We've outgrown it." He hooked his thumbs into the belt loops of his jeans. "And I'm only talking about the traditional stuff. What you're attempting here is—Believe me, Cathy. Nobody will have any patience for some poor confused little kid with a burnt log for a freakin' dummy! That's for damn sure."

"I like them!" Cathy said, her braces glittering. "I do. I know you don't care what I like, Dad, but I like them. Ventriloquists make me happy." She squeezed Marilyn tighter. "And I'm gonna be a world-famous ventriloquist someday, whether you like it or not!"

"Honey," he moaned, "it's burnt wood." He chopped the blade of his hand through the air. "Am I the only one in this house who sees that? Just look at it, Cath. It doesn't even have a mouth or—or even a face!" He turned to me. "Gary, could you back me up here?"

"Join the dark side, Luke," I muttered.

My father twirled the lollipop stick in his mouth, ruminating. "I

don't get the attraction of ventriloquism. Really. I'm at a loss here."
He shoved his hands in his back pockets. "But okay, if you insist, I'll
buy you a real dummy—"

"Stop it!" Gawky, crazy-legged, swinging her pointed elbows,
Cathy ran out of the family room and stomped up the stairs, trailing
a pungent whiff of scorch behind her. We heard her bedroom door
slam shut overhead.

Still seated on the floor, I smiled at my father. Shrugging, I turned
up my palms, as if to say, "Pubescent girls: a mystery to us all." Overall
I felt pretty good about how things had turned out in our family. At
one time I was the biggest troublemaker around. I was a source of
constant concern. My parents' fear for my future was the mortar that
held the bricks of our family together. Now, Mom was staying at Aunt
Connie's house in Florida, trying not to snort cocaine with bikers.
Cathy had fetishized a piece of firewood. I was sitting pretty for once.

Stroking his goatee, that gingery hamster of hair on his face, my
father gazed out the family room window at our snowplowed subur-
ban street. Cathy's strange behavior had called into question so much
that he had taken for granted, including his own hipness. He was
thirty-eight years old, a marketing director for Studio Arena Theatre,
a job that allowed him to dress and act like an artist—ponytail, earrings, jeans—yet still collect a businessman's paycheck. He liked
avant-garde theater, but he was not cool enough to deal with the
grotesque in his own home. Standing at the window, he crunched into
the lollipop dreamily. Flakes of green candy clung to the inverted trian-
gle of hair beneath his lower lip. He would have welcomed my mother's
input in a situation like this. He looked down at me and frowned.
"And what do you find so damned amusing, Mister?"

Simple. I was pleased that for once I was not the one being yelled
at. Regardless of her sometimes curious whims, Cathy was a straight-
A student and I was not. She played her clarinet with a dramatic flair
that charmed adults and music teachers, and I couldn't even whistle.
She had won awards for academic excellence, and I was often stuck in
detention, which in my school was called JUG: Justice Under God. I
was forced to write "conduct" and "discipline" repeatedly in neat
columns on lined paper until my right hand and wrist throbbed
painfully. Father Timothy sat at his desk, scowling at me. So I was
actually elated to see Cathy challenged by the same type of patriar-

chal oppression that I had grown so accustomed to and had been forced to counteract with an elaborate system of snorts, guffaws, and, on occasion, feigned loss of hearing.

Recognizing my father's discomfort, I changed tactics. I wasn't sure if he had noted that, for once, we were on the same side. In my sweetest model-son voice, I said: "Cathy is behaving very badly . . . Isn't she, Father?" I motioned with my crooked forefinger so that he might bend down closer for a secret boy-to-man chat. "Your daughter is disobeying you," I said gravely. "So maybe a little physical discipline might not be out of place," I suggested. "A belt whip across the calves?" I raised my eyebrows, alternately lifting and dropping my hands to indicate the scales of justice. "Or a whack on the shoulder with an umbrella?"

"Stop it, Gary," Pops sighed, "that's terrible." He squatted before me like a baseball catcher, put his hands on my shoulders, and said, "Does she seem a little . . . Do you think Cathy's . . ."

"Spanking?" I said. "Good old spanking."

"All right, cut it out now. You're not helping matters."

"Cathy's in trouble here," I reminded him, "not me."

"Shut up, Gary," he growled. "This is serious. Does she ever talk to you about her school or her friends there?"

Cathy went to Kenmore Middle School. It had an enormous student body, close to four thousand kids, with a substantial population of headbangers, reprobates, gasoline-sniffers, Dungeons and Dragons freaks, sex addicts, and video arcade loonies, and my father thought that I might be prone to temptation there. I needed extra attention. The previous summer he'd found caffeine pills in my sock drawer. It concerned him. Pills at twelve meant heroin and LSD by sixteen. So I went to a Jesuit school where vigilante priests roamed the halls like disgruntled cops walking a beat. One in particular, Father Joe, who smelled like hot mustard and sweat socks, would stop me in the hall and ask an inane question so he could peer into my eyeballs to see if my pupils were dilated. To this day, I don't know if he recognized in me a future stoner and was trying desperately to prevent this terrible fate, or if all his excited talk about illicit substances and "what they could do to a boy" actually drove me to the hookah by the age of fourteen. I was so ready for marijuana when it was invented back in 1985.

"She's your sister, Gary. Aren't you concerned?" my father said.

"Don't yell at me. I hardly ever see her anymore." It was true. She walked to school with her girlfriends from the neighborhood, and I woke up an hour earlier to catch a bus to another zip code. It was dark as midnight each morning when I mounted the steps of the yellow bus.

He leaned closer. His nose was inches from mine. "Hey," he said, low. "I'm not yelling at you. Okay, pal?" He squeezed my collarbone lightly. I smelled the sour apple of his lollipop. "But I want you to stop talking like that. Cathy is your sister. You don't really want me to hurt her, do you?"

"Physical discipline," I murmured.

"Christ!" He turned away from me and walked out of the room. In the kitchen a cupboard door banged shut. "God, grant me the serenity . . ." he intoned. A moment later my father returned, his cheek bulging with fresh lollipop.

"I'm going to check on Cathy," I said, getting up from the floor.

"Okay." He nodded. "Good man," he called after me.

I climbed the stairs and knocked on Cathy's closed bedroom door. "Get lost, Gary," she sniffled. "I just wanna be alone."

I opened the door and stepped in. The campsite/bonfire aroma blended with all the other smells of her bedroom: damp towels and washcloths; nail polish remover; sticky bottles of cheap perfume spot-welded to the dresser; cherry and grape lip gloss. Sprawled chest-down on her bed, her ankles crossed up in the air behind her, Cathy was flicking carefully through a *Seventeen* magazine. The charred log, Marilyn, was reclining (face first? or on her back?) on the once-white pillowcase, just under Cathy's swaying feet. In the virginal setting of her bedroom this black log was as conspicuous and disconcerting as a man standing naked in traffic. I sat down on the gray-smudged pink comforter and placed my hand gently on her back.

"You're right, Cathy," I said solemnly. "Ventriloquists are cool."

She swung her face to me. "Really, Gary? Do you think so?"

"Definitely," I nodded.

"I've been practicing every night," she said. Her forehead was covered with dirty fingerprint swirls. "I'm getting better, too. I think I'm pretty good. Do you want to see me do a routine?"

The smell of scorch and the mystical word "puberty" coalesced in my mind. Cathy had been damaged. A dark shadow had passed over our house like a smoke-raveling zeppelin. It would come for me too, I understood. Nobody could pass through fire unscathed.

"Sure," I said. "Okay."

She propped the burnt log on her lap. The front of her oversized yellow T-shirt was sooty and streaked with grime, like some demented crossbreed of Charlie Brown and Pig-Pen. "Okay," she said. "Here goes." She took a deep breath and shouted, "It's a nice day today, isn't it, Marilyn?"

Cathy bounced her left knee once, hard, and ashes clumped to the rug. "Mm-hmm," she murmured in response. She shook Marilyn back and forth.

"Do you like going to junior high, Marilyn?" Cathy yelled.

"Mmmm," said Marilyn.

"That's good," Cathy laughed. "School is important. Will you be ready for high school next year?"

Marilyn thought about it for a moment, then answered definitively: "Mmmm."

Cathy stared at me with raised eyebrows. "So? . . . What do you think?" A loose strand of blonde hair fell over her eyes. She pushed her lower lip out and blew the curl back. Her face was filthy.

"Wow," I said.

"Right? I'm getting good at it!" Cathy searched my face with her gray-green eyes. "Remember I told you about when Mr. Charleston and Woody came to my school for assembly? They were really great and everybody loved it when Mr. Charleston drank that orange juice and Woody sang 'Feelings.'" She laughed and hugged Marilyn closer to her chest. "Ventriloquism makes me happy and it's, like, good and really really fun. Why can't he understand that?"

I patted her forearm. "Because sometimes Pops is a dick," I said.

Cathy smiled at me. I smiled back. And soon we both broke out snorting and cracking up. At that moment, we were as close as we had been since Mom left for Florida.

It didn't last.

"Hey Cath," I said, regaining my breath. "I know how we can use Marilyn for something really great."

"How?" she said uncertainly. A vertical crease appeared between her eyes.

"Well, what Pops needs, I think, is a little physical discipline." I nodded my head at this inevitable conclusion. "He's being very bad, isn't he? So maybe you could bake a chocolate cake." I raised my eyebrows alluringly. "And we'll crush the log inside it. He'll eat the cake and then he'll flop around on the kitchen floor and we'll cram his nostrils full of salty peanuts while he cries!"

"What?" Cathy blinked at me, self-righteous horror spreading on her face. The chasm between her thirteen years and my twelve seemed to widen immeasurably. "I'm not gonna feed Marilyn to Dad! What are you a maniac? It would kill him!"

"Well, we should tie him to the tree out back and pour honey and Kool-Aid all over him and then break an ant farm on his head." I laughed and reached for the dummy.

Cathy jumped up. "What are you talking about, Gary?" she cried, shielding Marilyn from me. "He's our father. Are you joking, or what?"

"Just forget it." I glared at a John Stamos poster on her wall. "I was only kidding."

Regrettably, in that instant, I saw that nothing had changed between us. What I had pinpointed as common ground for insurrection, Cathy regarded as an obstacle to be singularly overcome with fierce determination. She would be who she was and I would be who I was and no family squabble would ever be portentous enough to change that. Oh, Cathy could dabble in darkness, as if it were an educational field trip, she could press her cute little button nose to the bus window and snap photos with her camera, but when foolish, spontaneous and possibly fatal decisions were required, my sister invariably turned her back and went skipping toward the light. Cathy never understood my twelve-year-old world and I didn't have the patience to instruct her in its finer points. As far as I could tell, she was a lost cause. She would go to Kenmore West high school the following year and become involved with music clubs and parties. She would earn high grades and head off to a university in Boston. Her days as an innovative ventriloquist would be long forgotten.

That night I left my sister's bedroom with hardly a backward glance. I trotted down the carpeted stairs, kicked open the back door and hopped down the slushy cement steps. Snow crunched underneath my sneakers as I trudged across the driveway.

Bones was galloping around the backyard, his ears flapping. I noticed that he'd knocked over his water dish and had chewed up one of Pops' winter gloves. "Bones!" I said sharply. "Up to a little mischief again, are you, boy?" I shook my finger at him accusingly. His wet brown eyes flashed at the sight of me. "Maybe you need somebody to teach you some manners." Bones started panting and hopping around as I neared him. "Follow orders! Pay attention!" I shouted. "Get in the coat closet! Listen to Father Timothy!" I grabbed Bones' collar and yanked hard on it until he yelped. "What are you going to say?" I taunted him. "Who is going to believe you? What you need, I think, is a little physical discipline. Then you'll know how to behave."

But Bones, he didn't understand. He was just a puppy.

From Letter to Antonio Saura

Marcel Cohen

MARCEL COHEN ORIGINALLY WROTE THIS LETTER TO ANTONIO
SAURA *in Ladino, the language spoken by Sephardic Jews after the
expulsion from Spain in 1492. Also known as Judeo-Spanish or Djudyo,
Ladino is essentially fifteenth-century Spanish sprinkled with many
words from Turkish, Hebrew, Greek, Portuguese, and other languages;
for centuries, it was the lingua franca of Jewish communities through-
out the eastern Mediterranean, particularly in Turkey. As he explains in
this extract, Cohen, who was born in 1937, learned Ladino as a child
growing up in France.*

*Letter to Antonio Saura was first published in 1985 in Spain, with
drawings by Saura (1930–1998), who was one of Spain's most prominent
postwar painters. Subsequently, Cohen translated his Ladino original
into French and a bilingual edition appeared in France in 1997. What's
immediately striking about the French version (on which I have based
my translation) is that Cohen chose not to translate certain words, thus
leaving nuggets of Ladino embedded in the French text. (He did, how-
ever, provide a glossary, which is also extracted here.) Equally striking
are the differences between the Ladino and French versions. While the
French is generally a faithful translation of the original, there are points
at which Cohen introduces new phrases and ideas. If this can partly be
understood as a writer revising his own text, it also suggests that there
are two distinct authors at work here: the first writing in the language of
his childhood, with all the accompanying limitations of vocabulary, syn-
tax and rhetoric; the second writing as an educated, highly articulate*

adult, the author of numerous, finely crafted books that have earned him a respected place in contemporary French literature. If this book is an account of what it feels like to inhabit a dying idiom, as well as an evocation of a lost world, it is also a meditation on the doomed nature of every translation.

— Raphael Rubinstein

I.

Dear Antonio,

I'd like to write to you in Djudyo before the language of my ancestors is completely extinguished. You can't imagine, Antonio, what the death agony of a language is like. You seem to discover yourself alone, in silence. You're sikileoso without knowing why.

II.

What I'm going to record here is more or less what my mind retains of the five centuries that my ancestors spent in Turkey. I was born in Asnières, a suburb of Paris, and my parents were in their thirties when they came to live in France. They spoke French perfectly; at the time it was the language of all the Jews of the former Ottoman Empire. They learned it at an early age in the schools of the Alliance Israélite Universelle, then in Istanbul at the Lycée Français of Galata Sarail. How could they not have loved France? This didn't, by any means, stop them from speaking Djudyo at home, and so it was that in listening to them I was immersed in the language, without exactly speaking it myself.

III.

Antonio, to rediscover my words I have to close my eyes, and many expressions come back to me without my quite knowing how. What can I say to you with la yaka ("That doesn't come to la yaka," my grandmother used to say), with the expression "the cucumber's ass" which made us burst into laughter, with "son of a mamzer" and all the things that make you "lose your reason."

Words stampede. They vanish as quickly as they arrive. But what else can we expect of them? Really, they only tell us about smells, the distant sweetness of dondourma, of keftikas, of all those home-cooked delicacies. Ultimately, they just reflect nostalgia and the tragedies of the past. As soon as I glimpse them, words escape and die far away, like clouds in the sky.

IV.

The mother tongue: that's what we called what we spoke at home. Will this mother ever die, Antonio? In her, our past grows old; in her, we are completely present to ourselves. And, if words are our true domain, how could they not also be part of our future? How could we imagine that we could one day become mousafires to ourselves in our own tongue? In our deepest being we know very well that things don't die, or at least not the feelings that we have for them.

But when, day by day, this language crumbles, Antonio; when, in its death throes, it slowly dilutes in the mabul, while, alone in your room, you have to close your eyes to exhume a few scraps; when there is no longer anything to read in this tongue and no friends to speak it with; when the woman you live with looks at you like a sick man who is slowly losing what remains of your sanity, and you feel obliged to forget a little more of yourself; when, staring at her on certain days that the past comes back at you in fits and starts, you feel like a complete stranger, having never really shared a roof with her because an ocean separates the two of you; when, despite all your efforts, you are unable to reveal more than a part of yourself, then, Antonio, you must admit that death speaks through your mouth.

V.

Death speaks through your mouth . . . In fact, Antonio, I'm already dead. In universities today, all sorts of students, linguists and the merely curious are interested in Ladino. Entire books are devoted to the history of the Sephardim. How could I not seem like a fossil on display in a museum? Of course, everyone is extremely kind. Everything is perfectly organized. The mousafires approach politely and read the little label placed behind the glass that protects me. What does it say?

"Interesting specimen of a Sephardic man, miraculously discovered in Paris in the second half of the twentieth century. As you can observe, this sample is in perfectly preserved condition. Speaking Spanish rather poorly, from simple lack of practice, he still understands it without the least difficulty. Notice above all his hair, which is not dark like a Turk's. And note how his skin is very pale. This proves that he belongs to the group of dolichocephalic humans inhabiting the Iberian peninsula at the time of the Catholic kings. Visitors wishing to listen to the snippets of fifteenth-century ballads that he still retains faithfully in his memory should exercise respect and patience, since this specimen has a horror of appearing ridiculous. Don't forget that this rare specimen is a creature of a solitary nature."

Note to visitors: "This French-born Constantinopolite has the curious habit of subsisting only on steak frites and red wine. It's therefore inadvisable to offer him those sunflower seeds and fustuks that monkeys in zoos are so fond of."

VII.

You know, Antonio, all Salonicians are dethroned kings. Dethroned and ancient. You can see them in New York, Montreal, Paris, London, looking like birds whose wings have been clipped. "Ke jaber?" "Everything's fine!" Yet they beat against the bars of their cage. For them, the worst of all evils is forgetting. They remember the quays where they used to stroll with their trespil, the white tower called Beyas Koule by the Turks, the lime-bleached walls of the old city whose reflections trembled on the water. They remember the blue of the sea and the blue of the sky, the softness of the imbat, the cries of the seagulls, the bilbil in the woods, the horns of the ships coming into port, the long silvery waves when they went out again. They remember the taste of grilled fish, the smell of flowers, the summer nights when they strolled among the kiosks, the boat trips under moonlight with, as a sonorous backdrop, the distant music of a dancing party on board one of the great ships lit up at anchor, while tiny fish came to the surface for air. They remember the thirty-five kales that they attended over the centuries, depending on their place of origin: the kal of the Castilians and the kal of the Aragonese, the kal of the Mallorcans and the kal of the Portuguese. They remember the keys of their house in Toledo, in Cordoba or in Granada, which the fathers handed solemnly to their sons so that they would forget nothing of the past and also, though they never quite stated it, in the unlikely situation that mazal would one day allow them to return. They remembered rare doubloons, patakons, maravédis and écus saved since the expulsion from Spain, mounted in precious yadranes that the women, both mothers and daughters, wore with their Shabbat dresses. They know that their ancestors, at least until the end of the nineteenth century, made little effort to learn Greek or Turkish, convinced that they had inherited the most treasured language in the world, a sacred language that gushed forth as sweet as honey. They remember that in the seventeenth century, envoys from proud Louis XIV had to learn Djudyo to do business in Greece and Turkey; that the first books printed in the Ottoman Empire were in Ladino; that the sultans, pashas and vizirs who held that doctors were "assassins of healthy people" placed their confidence only in Jewish physicians, heirs to the doctors of Salamanca. They remember the first Zionists who found them digesting their Turkish delights, enjoying their kyef and reciting together old romances. "Useless to talk to them about Palestine," the Zionists inevitably concluded, "all they want to do is go back to Spain."

They remember, evoking the New Toledo that was Salonica, the splendor of this Mother of Israel in a Turkish land, its old-time riches, its savants and printers, its famous rabbis addressing their responsa to all the Jewish communities of Europe. They didn't see that their star could ever dim.

They remember . . . It would be better to say that very few still remember. Fifty-four thousand Salonicians died at Auschwitz, along with one-hundred thousand other Sephardim. Night and fog. Nacht und nebel. The sons of light were overshadowed by night.

VIII.

Night. Boot steps on the quays, at the corner of alleyways, in the patios that are so much like those of Toledo. Boot steps snap the last threads to the past. The old songs are covered up by the din of the trains.

"It was day, it was day,
Daytime not night,
When the beautiful youngsters
Went about their love affairs."

Night. Frozen plains. Trees seeking sunlight. All of Europe, frigid. The cities stretched out like old prostitutes. Cold. Shame when, from time to time, someone remembers again; shame smothered under the white cotton of winter.

"Some seduce with oranges,
Others with lemons
And others still with apples,
Which are the fruit of love."

Trains and more trains, disappearing across the wintry plains. Their whistle-blasts covering up the cries of all Europe.

"Sad, I proclaim them, the wretched
Thrown into these prisons.
They don't know when it's daytime,
And even less when night falls."

Trains rattling across the sterile plains, passing through kazales, bugakes lost in the night, in the night of boot steps and thousands of ears glued to the walls of the cattle cars, even now attentive to the slightest baying of a dog. Trains and more trains, and these last words for the sons of light: "Don't be afraid, janoumika, don't be afraid. Sleep and God will protect you."

IX.

And then, silence. The silence of a rebuilt Salonica where not a single Jew could still be found to say prayers, and the silence of those who no longer had the courage even to tell stories. "It's useless to talk to people who don't want to listen," my grandmother used to say.

Silence and, on certain days, for who knows what reason, the babbling of the past suddenly resurfaces, twisting and turning in the mind like a caged bird.

X.

Antonio, I often page through catalogues of your exhibitions. Fascinated, I can't stop looking, with a strange sense of unease. "Imaginary portraits," you call the faces that proliferate in your paintings. I don't think for even a moment that they are. For me, the "imaginary" is simply what we have forgotten. "You think you're joking, but, alas, you'll find out that it's all too true," my grandmother used to scold when she didn't appreciate my sense of humor. "Mutlak, promise your vava that you'll never say such things again."

Artists are kuturugis, Antonio. But their memories are sometimes so vast that their works draw on knowledge they don't even know they possess. Jews are just the same: they've seen everything, or almost. In any case, they always know more than they think, even when they think that they've forgotten everything. "If you want to know the true age of a Jew," Edmond Jabès used to say, "you have to add 5,000 years to his official one."

Would you like to know, Antonio, what my grandmother would have said in front of your paintings? "Who is this, Torquemada? And all these scowling Papists with their noses in their mouths, these Popes as black as coalmen—what do they want from us? They look like real bichimsizes. They're going to bring us bela. There's no place for horrors like this in a Jewish home. Explain to your friend Saura that we are Galicians. We don't understand a word of what he says."

My grandmother wouldn't have been wrong. Look at your paintings. They're impregnated with all the world's blackness. How to make her understand that this is the only way to exorcise it? "May God punish them as he has us," she would have sighed. The soytarizes that you show us, Antonio, I know them all too well. We have to go for their throats. We must enforkar them, send them all to the devil. You know how I would finally try to explain things to my grandmother? I'd use one of her favorite proverbs. "When the cat catches a mouse, he's not trying to make sure his father's soul will rest in peace—he wants to bite off the mouse's head."

XI.

Strange, Antonio . . . strange to speak to you for the first time in the name of the Shephardic Jew that I am, and also for the last time. In my bedroom, I close my eyes, lie in wait for the words of the past, feel them come back to me, little by little, flush them out as if with a fener, and know that in these words there is no room for lying: it's in the music of these words that I feel most myself. In these words, in this music, I rediscover not only the true weight of things but also the flashing reality of daylight.

There is not, there never will be, anything but a wavering that takes the place of reality since Judeo-Spanish dies with those who speak it. I never asked myself if I loved this language or those who gave it life; I was a part of them.

And now, agonizing in my language, I let the mousafires express themselves while I write at their dictation. It's they who write, they who read me. All I know is how to listen to what's said in this little corner of the world and to note it down on the page.

XII.

I wonder if I'm being clear when I evoke these mousafires who express themselves through me? Do you remember what Kafka said about the German language? He explained that his mother would never be a mutter because she had nothing in common with Teutonic mothers. This is why Kafka felt he was totally incapable of evoking his mother in his writings.

That's my case exactly. My madre wasn't a mère, nor was my nona a grandmother. Between the madre, or mama, of the Sephardim and the French mère, between all the sweetness of a nona or a vava and that of a grand-mère, are five centuries of life in the Ottoman Empire which sink into the unsayable.

Translated from the French by Raphael Rubinstein.

Aradaboul: (Turkish) imaginary country.
Bela: (Turkish) misfortune, worries.
Bichimsiz: (Turkish) antipathetical, a bad guy.
Bilbil: (Turkish) nightingale.
Bugak: (Turkish) a backwater town
Djudyo: Jewish, but also, familiarly, Judeo-Spanish.
Dondourma: (Turkish) crème glacée.
Enforkar: (Portuguese) hang on the gallows.
Fener: (Turkish) lantern.
Fustuk: (Turkish) pistachio nut.
Imbat: (Turkish) sea breeze.
Jaber: (Turkish) information, news. Ke jaber?: How is it going?
Janoumika: (Turkish) diminutive of Janoum (the sultan's favorite), dear.
Kal: (Hebrew) synagogue.
Kazales: (Portuguese) villages.
Keftikas: (Turkish) meatballs.
Kuturugi: (Turkish) impulsive, imaginative.
Kyef: (Turkish) rest, good times, pleasure.
Mabul: (Hebrew) deluge.
Mamzer: (Hebrew) bastard.
Mazal: (Hebrew) chance.
Mousafir: (Turkish) foreigner, visitor.
Mutlak: (Turkish) faultless, irrevocable.
Sikileoso: (Turkish) anxious, oppressed.
Soytariz: (Turkish) juggler, buffoon.
Trespil: (Turkish) string of amber beads.
Vava: (Greek) grandmother (familiar)
Yadran: (Turkish) necklace.
Yaka: (Turkish) neck.

"I love my wife," he said, shrugging. "She's Russian," he added. (DeMarinis, page 185)

Drawings

Bruno Schleinstein

Harlekin

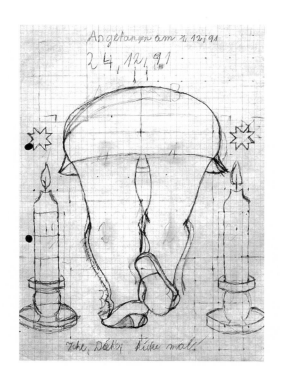

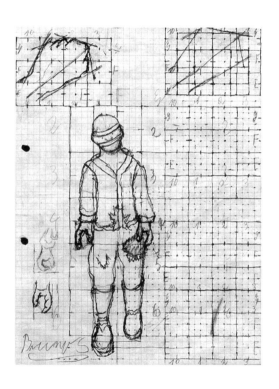

DAS WAR IN
SCHÖNEBERG
IN MONAT
MAI

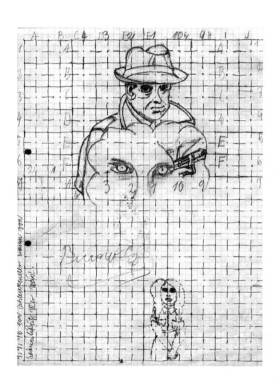

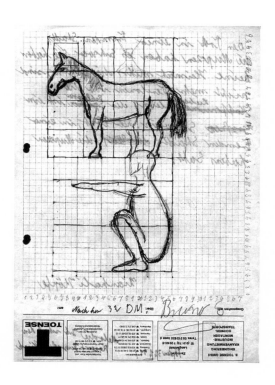

Der Tod in einer fremden Stadt,
die Musen haben es schwer, sie haben
keine Heimat mehr, die Eltern sind
nicht mehr ~~Verlassen~~ ist die
~~Heimat~~ lieber Eltern, der ~~Schlepper~~ ist ein
~~Geschäfte~~ Schwein! Der Tod in einer
fremden Stadt, ~~der~~ die Musen
haben Satt!

5, 15 49, 33 3 49 4

7439998

Dreinhalt Köpfe

3,— DM

Melodie Ich schreib den
Rosen ... ? Kirsch

B. den 32.4.99

Reliable Alchemy

Marcelle Clements

IT WAS THE MID-1980S, THE VERY END OF THAT ERA (OR MAYBE slightly past it) in which people unskeptically believed they would go out and, as a result of some unspecified but reliable alchemy of the New York night, reach a state of excitement, well-being, and curiosity about the rest of the evening that they would describe as having had a great time. Now in this new unidentified transitional phase, most people no longer had a great time, but few had begun to keep track of how much they drank or how much money they spent on unnecessary items or whom they flirted with and why. Women who were Susie and Kay's age, heading toward the end of their thirties, had not yet begun to lean in toward the mirror to study the furrows between their brows. Most men and women who remained—or had once again become—unattached, as it was termed, still assumed they could fall in love and become the heroes and heroines of a story that would end well in an ordinary way. In this nebulous era, no one had any great theory about what was going on. The most obtrusive symptom that something profound had shifted was how oddly difficult it had become to have fun.

If people like Susie and Kay talked about this in a half-worried sort of way, which was increasingly frequent, it was difficult to ascertain whether the city had changed, or whether they had. It certainly wasn't just a question of aging. These two, who had been roommates at Sarah Lawrence a little over two decades ago, still recalled (though they had never envisioned then that those days would ever be worth remembering), in their senior year, driving down to Manhattan in the evening, past all the late-night bars and restaurants they had heard about where people they had heard about were said to be drinking and dining. Those were people the same age then as they were now, people with jobs and children, who could not have imagined a life in which they didn't go out several times a week, for no other reason but to have fun.

In the spring and summer especially, the promise of the city's invitation was so lasciviously intense, so glamorous and cool, that the two twenty-year-olds could not bear returning to campus. They were entranced. At midnight, one, two, three in the morning, long after the other girls in their dorm, wearing nightgowns and knee socks, and drinking soup out of mugs, had finished their talk in the common room, rinsed off the cutlery, and gone to bed, Susie and Kay were still cruising around the city, collecting glimpses and glimmers of the life inside these places, which they imagined to be infinitely amusing, meanwhile growing more and more susceptible to the voluptuous appeal of the warm gray streets tinted by red, by green, by yellow, by red again, under the perennially violet Manhattan night sky.

What they had identified was a crowd of sorts, though it didn't think of itself as one, composed of people who would have been said to be in The Arts. They were not just downtown, but rather scattered here and there, in the Village and uptown, east, and west. Many people went from place to place on a whim, and at that time any person in this crowd could be found and easily met by anyone who really wanted to. If anyone had analyzed that social layer of Manhattan, it could have been said to be composed of a number of bubbles, each containing a subculture. Some were scruffy and dedicated to Art, like the bubbles belonging to painters, solo performers, modern dancers. Others contained those who were consumed by a Kilroy Was Here urge, innumerable screenwriters, for example, who mixed with journalists, graphic artists, directors, and some of the more monied actors, choreographers, an occasional costume designer, art historians, a classical cellist, several bebop piano players, a saxophone player or two—one of whom was also a stockbroker. All together, they added up to a fairly elegant and ironic beau monde that was as close as New York ever came to having a café society, at least in living memory. The fates of these pretty people turned out to be extremely varied: some were obsessed with what they called success, some only longed for proximity to it, while others sincerely disdained it. Some had made a great deal of money; others had not, yet they lived fancy lives, no one really knew how or on what, as if they were on a floating planet that hovered just above Manhattan, where a floating bank supplied them with enough glitter to fulfill all their needs. Some were socialites and took everything for granted, and others had escaped small town working-class lives just because they were talented, and still couldn't get over it. They were not a community (though the same people later imagined they had been) because they felt no loyalty to one another, until it was all over and it was too late. They were an ephemeral milieu, emitting the siren call of a social world with no basis in social reality.

By the time they settled in Manhattan, Susie and Kay's generation was cheated out of its due: This milieu, to which they had a natural entrée, was dematerializing faster than anyone could keep track as the considerably less fun real world was regaining its dominance. No one could have said precisely when the festive feeling had ended, nothing specific could be seen to have gotten broken or dissolved, or else too many things had to be counted. It had precisely the arc that is followed by a big party's soundtrack, when all goes well, in which initial chitchat swells to the hubbub of many conversations, growing fuller and less textured with each arrival until at the party's height, there is a wild din, crazily loud for the moment of its acme, when no individual sound is distinguishable anymore save for an occasional egregiously piercing shriek of laughter, when the party has lost consciousness of itself, and people loudly say, "Excuse me?" over their drinks so that their interlocutors will repeat the last remark. And then one person leaves and then another and then a whole lot and then another lot and then there are only a few people left, complimenting the hosts, and then the last stragglers take their leave, and then the hosts sit down and look at one another, surprised by the swiftness with which the zany whirlwind untwirled itself, and by the silence. There is nothing in auditory consciousness more startling, more uneasy-making and disorienting than the so-called silence that follows a loud, complicated, and sustained noise.

"Dagmar saw you, boy!" Dagmar saw you, boy! That kid said exactly that. I swear it! I spun around like an insane top. I looked everywhere. I looked in the water around the float. I scanned the far sides of the pool, and the grassy slopes. Dagmar saw you, boy. When I looked back for the kid he was gone. But that boy had been real, and he had said those exact words full of more wonder than any other words of my childhood. I swear it. (Kinder, page 31)

There Are Jews in My House

Lara Vapnyar

GALINA CARRIED IN AN ALUMINUM POT OF BOILED POTATOES, holding it by the handles with a kitchen towel. She put it on a wooden holder in the middle of a round table covered with a beige oilcloth. She opened the lid and, turning her face away from the steam, ladled coarse, unpeeled potatoes onto each of the four plates. The plates were beautiful: delicate, white, with a golden rim and little forget-me-nots in the center.

For the past six weeks, they'd been eating in the living room, where the heavy dark brown curtains covered the only window. For the past two weeks, they'd been eating in silence. From time to time, somebody coughed or sneezed, the girls might whisper something to each other, or even giggle, after which they glanced guiltily at their mothers, but mostly they heard only themselves blowing on their food and the clatter of heavy silver forks. Galina didn't mind the silence. It was better than having to talk, to keep up a forced conversation, as she did a few weeks before. Even the room itself was best suited for silence. It was large and square, empty and spotless. The sparse furniture was drawn close to the walls, and there was only a massive dinner table in the middle, rising like an island on the dark brown floorboards.

Since they dined on potatoes everyday, Galina was used to everybody's eating habits. Her seven-year-old daughter, Tanya, cut the potato in half and bit the insides out of the skin hurriedly, then ate the skins too. Raya, sitting across from Galina, peeled potatoes for herself and her eight-year-old daughter, Leeza. "Two princesses,"

Galina thought. Raya peeled potatoes with her hands, using her delicate fingernails to hook the skins. She bent her head so low that her dingy hair almost touched her plate. Raya and Leeza broke their peeled potatoes into small pieces and ate, picking them up with a fork. Raya's hands were often shaking, and then the fork clutched in her fingers was shaking too, knocking on the plate with an unnerving tinkling sound. Galina had the urge to catch that trembling fork and hold it tight, not to let it shake. "Chew, chew!" Galina kept saying to Tanya, who tended to swallow big chunks in a hungry rush. "You're wasting your food when you're not chewing." Galina herself ate slowly. She picked up a whole potato on a fork and ate it with the skin, biting off pieces with her strong, wide teeth. She chewed zealously, careful not to waste food and also trying to prolong dinner as much as possible, because the hours between dinner and going to bed were the most unbearable.

Six weeks ago, when Raya and Leeza first came to live at Galina's place, it had been different. Galina and Raya spent the evenings talking, mostly about the prewar life that seemed now unreal and perfect. They retold some minor episodes in meticulous detail, as if the precision of their memories could turn that prewar life into something real, and failure to remember something could unlock the door of Galina's apartment and let the war in. If one of them was unsure of a detail, she relied on the memory of the other. "I used to buy Moscow rolls every Saturday. Remember Moscow rolls, the small ones with the striped crust? They were six kopecks each. Were they six kopecks?" "I think they were seven—the ones with poppy seeds cost six." Often, their conversations went on well into the night, after the girls had fallen asleep. Then they moved closer to each other and spoke in whispers.

Now, right after dinner, Raya went into the back room, where she and Leeza slept, and sat on the bed with her back to Galina. Sometimes, Raya bent over the nightstand and started a letter—to her husband no doubt—but after a few lines she always stopped and crumpled the paper. At other times, Raya had a book in her hands, but she didn't turn the pages. Through the opened door—Raya never shut the door—Galina saw Raya's pale, unclean neck, so thin that you could count every vertebrae. Galina couldn't concentrate on a book either. She would follow the lines to the bottom of the page and only then realize that the letters didn't form words and sentences, but simply passed in front of her eyes like endless rows of black beads.

Galina dried the dishes and stacked them in the cupboard above her head. She put the aluminum pot on the lower shelf, shoving it deeper with her foot, then shut the cupboard door with a bang. She wondered if Raya heard the clatter. Sharp sounds made Raya shudder—a fork falling on the floor, a door's squeak, somebody sneezing, the toilet flushing. For a long time, Galina had tried to do everything as quietly as possible. Now she didn't care. Raya herself was quiet as a mouse. That's what she told Galina when she came: "I'll be quiet as a mouse." Galina wondered where this expression came from, why mice were considered so quiet. Because they weren't. Galina grew up in the country, and there were a lot of mice in their house. At night, they made distinctive mice sounds—scratching and nibbling and knocking against the floor with their tiny claws when they ran from one corner to another. Little Galina lay in bed thinking that if she opened her eyes she would see a mouse with crooked yellow teeth and moist eyes staring right at her.

Galina went into the living room, removing her wet apron. The usual picture: the girls on the sofa, making a dress for Leeza's doll from scraps. As always, Tanya was doing all the work and Leeza was giving instructions, Galina thought with annoyance. The doll's pink, shiny body was turning swiftly in Tanya's hands as she dressed her. It was a beautiful, expensive doll with the torso made from hard plastic and the head and limbs from some other, softer kind. It had blonde hair shaped into long, springy curls and round light-blue eyes that seemed to stare right at you. Galina didn't have toys like that as a child, and she couldn't afford to buy them for Tanya.

Galina peeked into the back room. Raya didn't turn to her, only bent lower. She was scribbling something with Galina's rusty ink pen. The pen was almost dry and made heart-rending sounds, scratching the paper.

Galina covered her ears and looked around. She had always liked that her room was so plain. There weren't any crocheted doilies, marble elephants, or crystal vases. The windowsills weren't decorated with pots of geraniums, the floors with rugs, or the walls with framed paintings. She didn't even have an image of the Madonna in the corner where it always hung in her mother's house. The only thing on the wall was a framed black-and-white photograph of Galina's mother. Now, Galina wished they had a painting—any painting, something to rest her gaze on. She uncovered her ears and immediately heard the awful scratching sound of Raya's pen, Leeza's troubled breathing, the snapping of the big tailor's scissors in Tanya's hands, Leeza's cackling cough. Galina wanted to open her mouth and scream at the top of her lungs.

She rushed to the hall, mumbling that she was going to get some air before curfew. She wondered if Raya heard her. She probably didn't. Because if she did, she would have darted out of the back room, asking: "What? What did you just say? You're going where?" Her face would have been distorted and her voice faltering. During the last few days, it happened every time Galina went out of the house. Every time. When Galina went to the market in the morning, when she left to talk with one of the neighbors or their former coworkers, when she simply went out for a breath of fresh air, like today. Every time, when Galina touched the doorknob, she felt Raya's begging stare on her. She saw that Raya wanted to fall on her knees, to clutch the edge of Galina's dress and not let her go. But she didn't do it, she just stood in the doorway, shifting from one foot to the other, clasping the doorframe with yellowed fingers, clearing her throat to ask in her thin, trembling voice again and again: "Where're you going? When will you be back?"

Galina opened the door and glanced in the direction of the back room. Raya hadn't moved.

Galina walked downstairs, trying to resist an urge to run. Part of her was expecting Raya to rush out the door and grab her by the sleeve. A ridiculous thought. Galina knew that Raya would never so much as stick her head out. She walked to the door and pushed the cold iron handle down. The door gave in slowly, scratching the stone floor and making a tired screech, the last sound before the silence of the outside.

It was beginning to get dark, but still the contrast between the soft, dusky light of the street and the semidarkness of the staircase was great. Galina had to shield her eyes for a moment. Their deserted street, with a few pale stone buildings, a few leafless trees, and broad rough sidewalks, was wide and airy. Galina threw her head back and inhaled hungrily. At last, she could breathe!

The declaration of war with Germany three months ago, in June, although completely unexpected, didn't shake Galina. Somehow she didn't see the war as a great tragedy, as a disaster rushing into their lives and destroying everything. For her, it was more like an unwelcome change in her daily life, requiring some practical adjustments. Galina made her husband, Sergey, dig a big hole in the empty plot of land behind their building and construct a little cellar, while she was buying potatoes, drying them in sheets of newspaper, and storing them in big sacks. Galina also bought large quantities of salt, soap, oil, and matches; glued strips of paper to the windows to protect them from shells; made sure that she and Tanya had enough warm clothes; and determined the shortest route to the air-raid shelter, counting the number of steps. She didn't feel shaken—on the contrary, she felt energetic and alive, something that hadn't happened to her in a very long time. She also felt proud of being able to keep calm and make rational decisions, while everybone else seemed to lose their head. Galina didn't feel shaken even when she saw her husband off to the front. They were stuck in the middle of a crowd of men going to the front and the howling children and women who were clutching the men's coats. Sergey was silent. The only words he said were about Tanya, that it was good that Galina didn't let her come along, that it would have been too upsetting. Galina thought it was good, too. She saw a glimpse of Raya nearby, howling like the others, with her hands tightly locked on her husband's back. "Don't they understand?" Galina thought, starting to feel annoyed. "It's war. Men are supposed to go."

Toward the end of the summer, when there was a clear prospect of the town being occupied, the evacuation started. The factory equipment was packed hastily in plywood boxes and put on freight trains along with valuable workers and the families of those soldiers who were members of the Communist Party. All the others (families of non-Communist soldiers, retired workers, and invalids) were supposed to follow in a few days. But in a few days, the town was cut off. Galina and Raya stayed, because neither of their husbands was a Communist.

The prospect of staying in the occupied town seemed uncomfortable to Galina, but not catastrophic, especially since Soviet newspapers said that the Germans treated the civilian population with decency. She had read it just a few weeks before the war. Galina made more practical adjustments: she buried all her modest valuables in the ground next to the potato sacks, she bought more soap and matches, she got rid of Tanya's red tie and a folder full of newspaper clippings about Stalin. Galina managed to keep her calm.

Raya was another matter. As soon as it was announced that the town would be cut off, she went into a feverish, panicky state. She spent the whole first day running around the station, grasping at anyone who would talk to her, begging the railroad officials to take her and Leeza on a freight train, trying to convince them that trains must run, simply because she, Raya, must leave. She continued to do that until she was forced away from the station along with the crowd of other desperate people. But, unlike them, Raya didn't give up after that. She spent the following days running around the town, attempting unthinkable measures to get her and Leeza out of town. She tried to bribe some truck drivers to take them east. She tried to bribe a clerk in the city passport office to forge documents for them. She walked to the small villages to the south of town and asked everyone there if they could take her and Leeza out on horseback. When she came home from her day trips, the soles of her shoes were worn through and her feet rubbed raw. She slumped onto a couch and burst into hysterical sobs, unable to calm herself, even in front of Leeza. Raya was Jewish. That explained a lot of things, Galina thought.

The war had been going on for a few months, and rumors became the only source of more or less credible information. The rumors about Jews differed. Some said that when Germans occupied a new town, the first thing they did was to put all the Jews on cattle trains and ship them away. Others said that Germans didn't bother to ship Jews anywhere; they just drove them together to the edge of town or to a big ravine and shot them all. Everyone: men, women, and children. A few refugees from Kiev, where Raya's parents lived, added more ghastly details. Tanya began asking Galina: "Do they make Jews take off all their clothes? Underpants too? Do they throw all the Jews into a big pit and then burn them alive? Have they burned Leeza's grandma?" Galina told her to stop listening to nonsense. But Tanya wouldn't stop: "Do they also burn kids? Will they burn Leeza?" Galina told her to shut up. Raya also couldn't stop talking about that.

She was running around town, looking for refugees and asking them more and more questions. She said she was sure that they were telling the truth. She said she could feel that her mother was dead.

It was hard to imagine Raya's mother dead. Galina had met her once or twice when she came to visit Raya. She was a very vivacious old woman—too vivacious in Galina's opinion. She wore silly hats and painted her lips, even though her face looked so obviously old, all wrinkled and puffy. She laughed a lot, showing her gold caps, and kissed Leeza in public. Galina tried to imagine Raya's mother as part of a gray, screaming crowd. She tried to imagine her naked, trying to cover her fat, wrinkled body, still wearing her silly hat. Did the hat fall off her head when they shot her, or did it stay? Was Raya's mother's dead body lying in a pit, still attached to the hat?

It was Galina who found a solution for Raya. A peasant from a nearby village, a relative of Sergey, agreed to take Raya and Leeza in his wagon as far as the next town, toward the eastern border. On the night they were supposed to leave, Galina came to see Raya off. Only then, seeing Raya and Leeza both dressed in their winter coats though it was a warm Indian summer night, seeing Raya's bursting-at-the-seams suitcase and Leeza's doll sticking out of her backpack, seeing their sturdy shoes and their grave faces, did Galina understand how real it was? Raya was leaving, leaving their town and leaving Galina all alone. Galina had an urge to grab Raya's hand and hold it, squeezing it harder and harder. She actually made a step toward Raya, but instead of taking her hand, Galina took the suitcase and carried it downstairs, clutching its cold leather handle.

The road led Galina to the deserted tramlines. German officers and soldiers—there were only a few of them in their town—occupied brick buildings in the center, close to the City Hall. Here, in this remote part of town, the reality of the war wasn't so evident. There wasn't a grocery store or a movie theater nearby, and the area had always been deserted at that hour, after people had returned home from work.

It was very quiet. Galina had always associated war with noise: the swishing of missiles, explosions, the rumble of passing artillery, screams. But now it seemed that the outside world had been silenced around her. There were more disturbing signs of war inside Galina's apartment: the unplugged radio, the unpeeled potatoes, the traces of white paper on the windows, Raya's wary eyes, Raya's shaking hands, the sound of Raya's pen, the whole of Raya's being. Galina would never have imagined that it could be so hard to stand her presence.

Galina and Raya met three years earlier, when Raya had moved into the town with her family and gotten a job as a junior librarian in the central library. It was the same position that Galina held. They sat at adjacent desks, went to lunch at the same little café on the corner, shopped in the same grocery store, and took the same tram to get home. They couldn't help but become friends. At the beginning, their main topic of conversation was the similarities in their lives. They loved to find more and more of them and then laughed in amazement. They lived on the same street in identical two-room apartments. They had daughters of almost the same age. Their husbands worked as engineers in the town's big textile factory. They were both outsiders in this town, having moved here because of their husbands' jobs. Neither had relatives or friends here. Raya had lived all her life in Kiev; Galina was born in a small village, but she went to school in Moscow and later lived there. So they were both used to life in big cities and found the town and their neighbors and coworkers very dull. They both were born in the beginning of March. They even looked alike: pretty, slender women of medium height, with blue eyes and wavy blonde hair. Library customers often asked if they were sisters, making Raya shake with laughter and say that she had always wanted to have a sister. Once Raya talked Galina into buying identical dresses. They put them on in the Central Clothing Store's dressing room, and stood staring at each other in the large mirror. "We are twins!" Raya cried.

Another similarity was that they both passionately loved novels and often read them during working hours, causing puzzled looks from other library employees, who used working hours for knitting and chatting. Their favorite novel was *Anna Karenina* and, unlike everybody else, neither of them found the ending depressing. Raya said that for her the saddest part was the scene where Anna talked to her little son for the last time. "I cried for three hours straight," she said. "I would stop for a few minutes and then cry and cry again. My mother became panicky and wanted to run for the doctor," she added, laughing. "After that scene the rest of the novel simply couldn't touch me." Galina didn't cry when she read that scene or Anna's suicide scene. Galina felt paralyzed for days—paralyzed with envy for Anna Karenina. Anna could live a normal, stable life, but she chose not to. She opened the door and found a new, different life, where everything, even her suffering and death, was better than in her old life. Galina could almost visualize Anna opening the door—it was a heavy, rusty door, and Anna was pushing on it with her round shoulder. In Galina's life, there were no doors. Galina wondered if Raya could understand that.

Raya seemed to understand a lot of things. She understood when Galina told her about Sergey's drinking. Everybody else refused to understand how his drinking was a problem. "Does he beat you?" Other women asked, "Does he beat your daughter?" "Does he smash furniture and throw vases out of the window?" "Has he ever been found sleeping in a ditch?" No, Sergey had never done any of that. He was a quiet drunk—he came home every night, walked to his bed, shaking and staggering, and slumped down. The next morning, he woke up with a headache, and then he had an empty, dead expression in his eyes the whole day. He was also a shy, guilty drunk. When Galina asked where the money was that she had saved for Tanya's winter coat, his lips quivered and he turned away and swore in a trembling voice that it would never happen again. Other women didn't understand, maybe because their own husbands also drank and they weren't as shy and guilty as Sergey about it. Raya understood. She sat next to Galina and let her talk and cry, never interrupting her, never suggesting anything, only patting Galina's back from time to time and smiling at her softly. Raya also understood things that Galina had always considered private, her own, nonexistent for other people. There often were sparks of recognition, when Raya described feelings and thoughts that Galina secretly shared. That pleased Galina—she wasn't alone. But at the same time, it frightened and appalled her—she didn't want to be faced with the reflection of herself in Raya. Once Raya said that she didn't love her husband. "I mean I love him very much," she corrected herself hurriedly. "But I don't . . . really love him." "I often have this uneasy feeling when I am around Leeza," Raya said another time. "Often I see that she is forcing herself to talk to me. She's never like that with her father. Sometimes, I wonder if she loves me." Galina had wondered if her daughter loved her, too. She seemed to be so much closer to her father. When Sergey was sober, they spent time making model airplanes, or playing chess, or talking, bursting with laughter from time to time, but when Galina entered the room, their laughter always stopped abruptly. Galina tried to do things with Tanya, too, but something always went wrong—Tanya became restless in a few minutes and Galina annoyed. "Do you love your daughter?" Galina wanted to ask Raya, but she didn't. She was afraid to hear the answer.

They didn't always talk about serious matters. Often they got together to chat about their lives, to share family anecdotes, stories about their adolescent crushes, cooking recipes, and makeup secrets. Or rather it was Raya who shared her makeup secrets, because Galina didn't know much about that kind of thing. Raya also knew a lot of tricks about underwear: "Galina, darling, don't stuff the whole thing in, bras are not for hiding your breasts—they are for pushing them up"; or about feminine hygiene: "You see, this way it will never leak, it will never stain your skirt again." Galina's fascination at these remarks was mixed with embarrassment—she'd never had anyone talk to her that way before.

They began spending more and more time together. Raya would drop by on weekends or after work, before her husband came home. Sometimes she brought Leeza and left her to play with Tanya in the living room while she and Galina talked in the kitchen. Galina often had things to do, and Raya sat at the kitchen table with a teacup in her hands. Galina was moving about, wiping counters, scrubbing floors, cleaning carrots covered with layers of dirt, chopping gray chicken carcasses, or frying potatoes in a hissing skillet. When Sergey came home drunk, Galina got Tanya and they went to Raya's place to spend the evening. There they sat in Raya's messy kitchen and talked, often for hours. Raya never seemed to worry about cooking or cleaning. Galina thought that nothing, not even fire or flood, could distract Raya from talking. Once, Raya had a pot of soup boiling on the stove, white froth pushing from under the lid. Raya saw it, but she didn't go to turn off the gas until she had finished her sentence. While they talked at Raya's place, the girls were usually playing in the back room, and Misha, Raya's husband, was lying on the living room couch with a book. Sometimes, Misha came out into the kitchen and asked apologetically if there was something to eat. Raya would jump off her chair and say that she was sorry, and that she had forgotten all about dinner. She then began running around the kitchen trying to fix a meal—something very different from what was served in Galina's house. Dishes clattered, packages fell out of cupboards, and pieces of food dropped onto the floor. Sometimes, Galina stayed to help, and they cooked a meal together and then ate dinner together— all five of them.

The sidewalk was scattered with piles of slimy autumn leaves. They gave out a strange, sweetish smell when Galina touched them with her foot. Her toes were slowly getting chilly. Galina stepped over the glistening tram rails and started walking between the wooden ties. The dry gravel rustled under the thin soles of her boots. She had a pleasant prickly sensation in her feet every time she stepped on a little pebble. She didn't know where she was walking, just away from home, away from Raya.

Galina had never liked their dinners at Raya's place. She sensed that Raya and Misha were tense, and maybe a little embarrassed, because they had cheese and salami and canned sardines and early tomatoes on their table—things that Galina couldn't afford. Galina felt uncomfortable. Tanya's behavior made her feel even worse. She grabbed slices of salami from the plate—several slices at once—and said with her mouth full that she never thought "sausage" could be so delicious. She stuffed quartered tomatoes into her mouth, spurting red juice along with the seeds, and smiled happily. All of that in contrast with Leeza, who ate slowly, reluctantly, after being begged by Raya: "Darling, please, one more piece." Galina often felt the urge to smack Tanya on the back of her head, smack her hard, so that damned slice of salami would fall out of her mouth.

Misha's presence also made Galina uncomfortable. She avoided looking at him, probably because he was so unattractive, even ugly. Galina remembered how stricken she was when she saw Misha for the first time. Raya and Leeza had come over for Sergey's birthday, but Misha was late. When he came in, the apartment was already packed with people. He entered timidly, towering above the sea of heads and clouds of tobacco smoke. He searched the room with his eyes, looking lost, and Galina thought for a second that he'd come there by mistake, he looked so different from everyone else. Misha had a small torso and a small head and very long, clumsy limbs. His neck was also very long, his nose large and wide. Raya called him "my ugly gosling." Misha was a quiet man; while others were yelling, laughing, and later singing drunkenly, he sat in the corner with one of Sergey's technical magazines. When Raya appeared next to him, always out of nowhere, all flushed, intoxicated by the party atmosphere, he put his hand around her waist in a shy but at the same time proprietary way. She stroked his back, rubbed her face against his bony shoulder, said "You're my ugly gosling," and kissed him, making him blush and smile. Apparently, Galina thought, the ugliness in a man was something you could get used to. Otherwise, Raya wouldn't be able to kiss him, or stroke his back, or go to bed with him and enjoy it.

"Well, I enjoy it," Raya had once said, sitting in Galina's kitchen. "Misha's not bad . . . he does everything to give me pleasure." Raya sat on the windowsill with her feet dangling. Galina was on her knees, scrubbing her chipped wooden floor. The stirring of Raya's shoes in front of her face was very annoying. Then Raya bent down to Galina and said in a slow whisper, "But, you see, something's missing." Galina caught herself blushing all over. She mumbled something like "Really?" and dived under the table to continue scrubbing there.

"How is yours?" Raya asked once. Galina wasn't surprised by her question. She could feel that Raya longed to talk about that every time they chatted about the kids, shopping, and underwear. Galina had even prepared her answer. Deep sigh and shy smile. (She had seen an actress in a Western movie do exactly that, when asked a similar question.) "I bet," Raya said. "Your husband is so handsome!" Galina heard this a lot. She used to think him handsome, too. But with time, Galina started noticing the drawbacks in Sergey's appearance, more and more of them each year, and then nothing but drawbacks. Recently, she'd noticed that with his slightly protruding eyes and meaty lips, Sergey looked like a cow.

"He tries to give her pleasure," Galina often thought, while sitting across from Misha in Raya's kitchen. The very idea of trying to give each other pleasure was strange to Galina. Neither she nor her husband had ever had that intention. At first, when there was passion, they just did it in a way that seemed to be the simplest and the most obvious. They were like two hungry animals that gobbled up their food, not bothering to enhance the flavors or to serve it beautifully. And after a few years of marriage, especially since Sergey's drinking had intensified, their infrequent sex had been hardly about pleasure or even simple enjoyment. Sergey usually crawled into bed, sighed and whispered, "Let's put the stick in." "Some stick!" Galina thought. It was limp and looked more like a wrinkled old sock. It hurt when Sergey struggled to put it in. "Help me," he said plaintively. Galina helped him, trying not to look at his neck, reddened with effort, and his damp hair, unnaturally yellow in the moonlight. After that the bedsprings started squeaking with resentment, and Galina lay, squished by Sergey's heavy body, feeling his unshaven chin rubbing against her skin somewhere above her ear. She sometimes threw worried looks in the direction of Tanya's bed, but Tanya always slept soundly with her face buried between the pillow and the wall. In a few minutes, the squeaking was over and Galina hurried to the bathroom. When she returned, Sergey was fast asleep.

The high point of Galina's sex life came in the gynecologist's office, where she went for her annual checkup. The doctor, an unsmiling woman with a thin bun of greasy dark hair, never looked at her patients. She checked them quickly with a slightly disgusted expression, then sat down at her desk and buried herself in her papers. Galina knew that at some point the doctor would cough and ask, "Do you live . . . ?"—inquiring in this modest manner, whether a patient was sexually active. Galina always said yes. She did. She lived.

Galina's legs were aching—she must have walked a long distance. A few feet away, she saw the bright red lettered sign of the Central Clothing Store. ODEZHDA. Actually, the letters D and E had fallen off, and the sign looked like a mouth with missing teeth. Galina walked to the entrance, stepping over shards of broken glass. The store's glass window had been broken, and what had been inside stolen or ravaged—the work of looters. She peeked inside, careful not to cut herself on the shards of glass. Torn boxes, pieces of cloth, a few metal dress racks, plastic hangers, and buttons—hundreds of buttons— were scattered all over the stone floor. White plastic dummies stripped of clothes, with their bald heads and gray felt torsos, were lying on their backs by the gaping holes that had once been windows. Further into the store, Galina saw the door to the fitting room hanging on one hinge, and inside the fitting room, a shattered mirror.

That day when Galina and Raya were changing into the identical new dresses in that very fitting room, Galina had been in a hurry to put her dress on, because she didn't want Raya to see her ugly woolen underwear. She threw the dress over her head and wiggled her body to pull it down. The zipper got stuck, and Raya, who was still in her underwear, came up to help. Galina felt Raya's sharp little fingernails tickling her back as she was yanking up the zipper. It was chilly in there, and they were giggling from cold and excitement.

The dresses were made of light cotton, dark blue with specks of white and red. They had short sleeves, low necklines, and fringed hems. "We are twins!" Raya cried when they both looked in the mirror, but Galina saw that the identical dresses, instead of making them more alike, pointed out the differences. Raya's face had more color. Her skin was very white, her cheeks rosy, her blonde hair lighter than Galina's, and her eyes were a brighter shade of blue—Galina's were almost gray. Or maybe it was Raya's beautiful turquoise earrings that made her eyes seem so blue. Galina saw that her own features were regular and well defined, when everything on Raya's face was smooth and diffused: puffy eyelids, plump cheeks without a cheekbone line, soft mouth. Galina tried to figure out what the shape of Raya's nose reminded her of. Then she saw it: a big raindrop, narrow at the top, rounded and wide at the tip. Galina smoothed the folds of fabric over her chest and straightened her back. Her breasts were firm, her shoulders broad, her legs shapely and muscular. Her whole body was finely molded, if a little square. Raya's figure seemed to be made of imperfections. She had thin calves and forearms, but her upper arms and thighs were plump. In addition to that, Galina had seen a glimpse of belly hanging above Raya's silk underpants when they were changing. No matter how elegant and expensive those underpants were, they couldn't conceal the soft white bags of excessive flesh.

Galina was called beautiful more often than Raya. One man in the library even said that she was a pure example of Slavic beauty and that he had seen a painting that looked exactly like Galina in one of the art books. The man was very old. His fluffy white beard touched the pages of the book when he was leafing through it, trying to find the painting for Galina. When he found the page, they saw that it wasn't a painting, but a marble sculpture called simply *A Slavic*

Woman. Galina agreed that there was a striking resemblance. The same hard upturned nose, the same prominent cheekbones, the same firm, finely carved lips. The woman from the book was beautiful, and so was Galina. But men always noticed imperfect Raya first. Raya smiled a lot, Raya shrieked, Raya squinted her eyes, Raya painted her lips bright red, Raya rocked her hips, Raya talked sweetly to every man that walked into the library, Raya wore high heels and shiny narrow belts fastened too tight on her plump waist. "A little whore," as Galina's mother would have said.

For some reason, Galina's mother had been turning up in her thoughts more often since the war began. Galina didn't think about her with defiance, the way she used to before her mother's death and for a long time after that. Instead, she tried to imagine how her mother would have reacted to one event or another in Galina's life. Galina tried to bring up the memories of the time that they spent together, to recall her mother's words, the sound of her voice, her facial expressions. Most often, she thought of their Easter walks to the cemetery, maybe because that holiday seemed to soften her mother, and that was when Galina felt closest to her. Galina was holding her mother's hand as they walked to the village cemetery along with the cheerful crowd of smartly dressed, drunk, overheated people, who carried brightly colored paper flowers, dyed eggs, bottles of vodka, and Easter cakes. The crowd squeezed through the iron gates, then spilled into the cemetery to eat and drink on the graves of their relatives. The grave she and her mother visited was in the last row, by the fence. There were very few other people in their corner. They spread their food on a little bench where Galina's grandparents, her father, and her baby brother had been buried. Galina didn't remember any of them, and she wasn't sad; she liked the gay colors of dyed eggs and paper flowers, the taste of sweet, crumbling cake, the quiet of the place. Galina's mother didn't talk much, except this one time, when she had had a little more to drink. "Look there, Galina," she said, pointing her rough brown hand in the direction of the fence that separated the Christian cemetery from the Jewish one. Her face was flushed and her eyes glistened. "Those are Jewish graves. Look at them. And then look at ours." Galina stood up, shaking the crumbs off her starched Easter dress, and walked to the fence. There she moved the dense branches of a young maple tree away from her face and looked. "Look what Jews have, daughter," Galina's mother repeated. She saw iron fences painted black, and inside the fences, fragile shoots of young violets and forget-me-nots struggling through the heavy, dark soil. She saw gravestones—they were small, but made of real stone, each of them with a crooked, wrongly shaped star. "Now look what we have." Galina stepped away from the fence and looked around: lopsided crosses made of rotting wood, paper wreaths, and eggshell, a sea of colored eggshell. On the way back, Galina was tired and sleepy and had to lean on her mother's hip. Her mother's words were coming from above and seemed to bundle up Galina's head like a heavy, warm shawl. "Remember, Galina. Jews get everything. They have ways."

Galina wondered what her mother would have thought if she knew that Galina was hiding Jews in her own home.

On the night when Raya was supposed to leave with the peasant, she appeared at Galina's door at about 3 A.M. She stood in the doorway in her boots, caked with country mud, soaked with sweat under her winter coat, and shivering. She said that they had come to the road crossing as had been agreed and had waited there until two, but the peasant didn't come. Galina tried hard to hide her initial happy reaction on seeing Raya again. She could barely listen to Raya's words: "I saw Russian troops. They were running. Running!" They were jumping over the fences, she said; most of them didn't even have their guns or rifles. They were trying to tear their uniforms off as they ran. "This is the end," Raya said. "We're going to die." There was a weird, agitated expression on her face. She seemed to be waiting for something. Her eyelids were twitching, and she was rubbing them with the back of her hand. "Calm down. This is not the end," Galina said. They stood in silence for a few minutes.

There were dabs of mud on Galina's spotless doormat after Raya left. Galina picked it up and went to the sink to wash it.

"The Germans will be in town soon, very soon," Galina thought as thin streams of brown water ran into the sink off the doormat. "They may even come today. If you believe the refugees, it will be a matter of days before they'll round up the Jews." Her hands were getting cold; she shook the water off the doormat and carried it back to the hall. "Raya may be dead in a few days," she thought. Both Raya and Leeza. Galina sat down, making the chair screech. Tanya shifted in her sleep, and Galina rose to pull up her blanket. They will be dead unless they come here. Galina's heart was pounding, but her mind suddenly became very clear. Everybody they knew thought that Raya was going to leave with the peasant. Just a few families remained on their street since the evacuation, and there was very little chance that somebody had seen Raya returning tonight. If Raya and Leeza stayed in Galina's back room and never left her apartment, nobody would ever see them. Tanya was very smart for her age; Galina knew that she wouldn't talk. The people who used to drop by Galina's place before the war—mostly Sergey's friends—were all gone. Nobody could inform on them to the Germans. And if the Germans decided to look for Jews in houses, they would hardly make it to Galina's remote part of the town. There still was danger, of course. Great danger. But the thought of the danger didn't dampen Galina's ardor; on the contrary, it made her all the more enthusiastic.

Galina didn't remember ever being as excited as she was, running to Raya's place. They had to make it to her place before dawn. "Grab your things and come to my place. We have to make it before morning," she said breathlessly to Raya as soon as she entered her dark hall. Raya, still fully dressed, but without her coat, rushed up to Galina and burst out sobbing. She mumbled something rapidly while clenching Galina's shoulders. The words coming from her mouth seemed to be drenched with snot. They were hard to make out. They were about the great risk for Galina and Tanya, and that Raya couldn't accept this, that she and Leeza had better try to sneak out of the town, walk to the woods and hide there, and then again about the sacrifice, the great risk for Galina and that she couldn't accept it. Galina felt Raya's sharp chin and sticky tears on her shoulder. She had the urge to dry herself, but she had to wait until Raya was through. She knew that Raya's tears were sincere, but at the same time she sensed that her little speech had been prepared. She glanced around the room and saw Raya's unpacked suitcase by the door, her coat, dropped on the chair, and Leeza, also still fully clothed, hunched in the corner of the sofa. Galina saw that her invitation had been expected for a long time and already accepted. She felt her excitement fading.

Later, Raya and Leeza stood silently in the hall of Galina's apartment. Raya had been at Galina's place hundreds of times before and knew her way around it. When Galina threw birthday parties, Raya, who always came early to help, was rushing from the kitchen to the living room and back, helping Galina to set the table and bring the dishes in. And when the guests came, Raya met them in the hall and told them where to put their coats and led them cheerfully into the living room. Now she stood barefoot on the blue, knitted doormat— she had just taken off her boots—asking where to put Leeza's and her coats. Galina gave them slippers and led them to the back room. They went there timidly and sat on the bed. Tanya, who had been woken up and told everything, sat in her bed, trying hard to look serious and adultlike. Nobody knew what to do next. Galina looked at Leeza's sharp shoulders under a checkered dress, Raya's hands folded between her knees. These two lives were now completely dependent on her; their very existence was in her hands. Galina desperately wanted to back out, to say: "No, no, you can't stay here. It's not for me. I am the wrong type of person. I am not prepared." But it was too late to change anything.

Galina walked away from the clothing store. Her legs and back had become stiff. She made a few hard, quick steps to warm her feet. As she was stomping her feet on the rough surface of the sidewalk, Galina had an unnerving feeling that Raya was somewhere nearby. That she had followed her all the way from home and was standing, hidden somewhere, behind a lamppost or a former beer stall. Galina even took a quick look around, but of course there was nobody there.

A few feet further down, she saw an abandoned tramcar. It stood on the rails with the doors open, as if it had just stopped and was waiting for the passengers to get in. There was something very peaceful about it. Galina walked to the closest door and climbed inside. It didn't bother her that all the light bulbs had been unscrewed and the windows removed, along with most of the seats. Galina made her way to the back and sat there on one of the remaining seats. She thought that if she closed her eyes she might hear the tramcar's bell and it would start off with a jolt. And then Raya would start talking. For some reason, when they used to ride together, Raya talked only when the tram was in motion. When the tram made stops, Raya also stopped abruptly and waited until it resumed. That was how Galina heard about Raya's love affair, between tram stops.

"I think that man likes me," Raya said. Her feverish whisper was mingled with the rattling wheels and the crackling of the tram's wires. "That man, from the library, did you notice him?"

Galina had noticed. A man had come to their corner and asked if they had some reference books on hydromechanics. A new face in town, probably an engineer on a business trip. A rather unimpressive man, in his late forties, short, balding, with a neat, round belly rising above his trouser's belt. Raya blushed and offered to show him the shelf. She walked ahead of him, and Galina could see that Raya tried a little too hard to straighten her back and make her hips rock smoothly. The reference books were on the upper shelf. Raya had to climb up the ladder. When she stepped down, the man gave her his hand, but she stumbled (on purpose, Galina was sure of that) and laughed as playfully as she could.

Raya wiggled in her seat and sighed: "He has beautiful eyes, doesn't he? And his mouth . . ."

Ordinary eyes, Galina thought. Small, dark. She tried to remember his mouth. He had full, bright lips, the kind that were usually described as sensual in novels. Did that make him a good kisser? "I wonder how his kisses feel," said Raya, and Galina flinched at the similarity of their thoughts.

And then, when they were squeezing through the crowd to the exit, Raya whispered: "You know what he said to me?" Galina shrugged. Raya leaned close to her and Galina could hear her fast, excited breathing and feel the faint, unpleasant smell of her lipstick. "He said that, when I was standing on the ladder, he could see the contours of my underpants through my dress, and he couldn't take his eyes off them!"

Galina was stunned. She couldn't stop thinking about that all the way home from the tram stop, and later, while she was preparing dinner and waiting for Sergey to come home. Her roommates in college used to talk about their boyfriends all the time, but their talk was coarse and direct: "He came by last night. We fucked." That didn't move or embarrass Galina. This was different. Galina couldn't quite understand how it was different, but she knew that she didn't want to hear it. She couldn't avoid it though. Whenever they got together, at work, during lunch hour, when Raya dropped in for a cup of tea, while riding the tram, Raya talked about her engineer. There were times when she caught Galina's disapproving look, or grin, or flinching. Galina couldn't hide her attitude completely, and Raya wasn't so insensitive as to ignore it, but she simply couldn't stop: she was bursting with stories and details she had to tell; she'd become addicted to telling.

One of Raya's last revelations was made in a tiny café called Meat Patties, where Galina and Raya went on their lunch break. Galina remembered every detail about that day. They stood at the tall, round table with one iron leg—there were no chairs in the café—in front of the big dirty window. Galina had a thick glass in front of her filled with "coffee beverage"—a sweet grayish liquid lacking both coffee flavor and aroma. Raya was holding an identical glass, but filled with beef broth. There was a chipped white plate with two patties on the table along with Raya's shiny black purse. Raya nibbled on her patty, having just told Galina the latest developments in her affair. Then she put the patty down and licked the crumbs off her lips with a dreamy smile. "You know what he told me yesterday?" she asked. Galina silently groaned, preparing to hear another sloppy compliment, but she wasn't prepared for this. "He said"—Raya said it slowly, emphasizing every word—"that my 'you know'"—she glanced down at those words—"tastes like red currant jelly." Then she laughed. Galina felt her whole body go down, as if somebody very strong were dragging her to the floor, and at the same time she felt that the heavy, round table was tilting in her direction along with the patties, the glasses, and Raya's purse. She grabbed her glass instinctively, and when her dizzy spell—she figured later that it must have been a dizzy spell—began receding, she found herself still holding tight to her drink and Raya still laughing. The sensation couldn't have lasted more than a few seconds, but Galina felt ill and disoriented. She couldn't bear the sight of laughing Raya with her crooked teeth and the blue slits of her eyes. She suddenly felt an irresistible urge to throw her hot coffee into Raya's face, to hear her laughter replaced by a scream, to see her delicate features distorted by shock and horror, and see the streams of dirty liquid running down her pale cheeks. The urge was so strong that Galina caught herself raising her glass and pointing it in Raya's direction. She didn't throw it; instead, she found herself asking in a strange, coarse voice, feeling that her words weren't her own but dropped out of her mouth like heavy rocks: "Does it?" Raya stopped laughing. "Does it what?" "Taste like red currant jelly?" Raya laughed again, quieter this time: "How would I know?" she said.

That night, it was too hot to sleep. Galina lay in bed on top of the covers, fanning herself with the lacy ruff of her thin cotton nightgown. She could hear her daughter making quiet whistling sounds in her sleep and her husband snoring next to her. Galina tried to imagine how it would feel if a man did all those things to her. She tried to picture the boys who'd courted her in college, but she couldn't remember anything about them. All she saw was blurry gray figures without faces, wearing cheap student clothes. Yet she had a vivid image of Raya's lover, painfully clear, as if he were right here in bed with her. Everything that seemed ugly and revolting about him before was arousing now. She could feel his shameless red lips pressing into hers and crawling down her neck, she could feel his big, soft hairy stomach touching her legs. She could feel herself inhaling his unfamiliar breath and lifting up her nightgown for him. She could see his head—balding crown, framed with dark, wiry hair—moving between her legs. Galina slipped her hand down.

She hadn't done so in a long time, not since she was fifteen and her mother caught her at it. She still remembered her mother's coarse scream and her hard, very cold fingers groping her shoulder. She pushed Galina off the bed and dragged her, shivering and stumbling, to their big stone oven, where she grabbed Galina by the wrists and pressed her palms to the red-hot iron door. Galina remembered how afterward she sat on her bed, too shocked to cry, and her mother was greasing her burned palms with lard, crying and saying again and again, "Galina, I don't want you to become a whore."

Galina's eyes were closed, but she felt her mother staring at her now from her picture on the wall. "Yes, mother, yes," Galina thought, "look what I am doing! Maybe I want to be a whore. Maybe that's what I've always wanted!"

When it was over, Galina pushed back the damp bangs that stuck to her face and wiped the beads of sweat from her nose. Her hands were trembling and her heart was beating so fast that it nauseated her. Her mother's picture was barely visible in the moonlight, but Galina could still make out her tightly pressed thin lips, her carefully combed hair, parted in the middle, and her eyes. She suddenly noticed that her mother didn't have her usual severe expression in that photograph. She looked bewildered, as if a photographer had taken her by surprise; she looked frightened. Galina turned onto her side. The whistling sounds that her daughter made drove her crazy, like the buzzing of a bunch of mosquitoes. So did Sergey's bursts of snoring. He lay on his back now. His mouth was agape. He reeked of onions and vodka. Galina buried her head under a pillow and sobbed.

The next morning she was late for work. She woke up on time, but she lingered at home trying to put off the moment when she would have to see Raya. She knew that she wouldn't be able to listen to her stories today. Galina saw Sergey off to work and Tanya off to school, then went back to bed. She lay wrapped in a thick woolen blanket and thought about Raya. Her thoughts were different than before. They were full of hatred. She had felt some resentment or envy or maybe even anger before, but never this. She lay and wished that the most horrible things would happen to Raya. She wished that her husband would know about her affair and throw her out. She imagined Misha's long, awkward body shaking with sobs. She imagined pale, scrawny Leeza holding her father's hand, trying to comfort him. And she imagined Raya, on her knees in a doorway, begging them to let her stay. Misha wouldn't even look in her direction, and Leeza would only shake her head no. Maybe Misha would receive a letter from somebody telling him about the affair, or a phone call. A phone call would be better. Somebody should call him. It was so easy to pick up the phone and dial the number . . . Galina felt a cold sweat breaking out on her forehead. Maybe she was simply coming down with something. Maybe she had a fever. She took a thermometer out of the bedside drawer, shook it, and stuck it under her arm. Five minutes later, she inspected it and saw that her temperature was normal. Galina climbed off the bed and dragged herself to the bathroom. She turned on cold water and held her face under the tap for a few seconds, then she began dressing for work.

Raya wasn't at her desk. It was the first thing that Galina noticed when she walked into the library. The desk looked deserted, with Raya's broken pencils in the pink plastic cup and a small family photo, but without her scattered lollipops, the shiny purse, and her knitted cardigan thrown on the chair's back. For a second, Galina thought that her wishes had come true, that something horrible happened, that Raya's husband found out and that somehow it was all Galina's fault. Then the women in the library told her that Raya was okay, just taking a sick day to sit with her daughter. Galina felt relief at first, but then it became relief mixed with disappointment. Raya wasn't punished. "She got away," Galina thought. "She can have all she wants and get away with it."

A few days later, Raya came back. She looked thinner, had dark circles under her eyes, and smiled less. She said that her daughter had had a bad cold and the doctors suspected pneumonia, but the diagnosis wasn't confirmed. Then Raya added matter-of-factly that the engineer had gone back to Moscow and that she didn't care. "When your child is sick, you can't be bothered with this stuff." Galina could see that Raya was lying. She could see how tense Raya became every time the phone rang in the library, how she stared at the same spot on her desk until somebody answered the call and she heard that it wasn't for her. Raya didn't laugh as much as she had before. She didn't flirt with men—when they walked up to her table, she gave them a quick, sulky look the way all the library employees did. "He dumped her," Galina thought, liking the sound of the word. "Dumped, dumped, dumped." A rubber ball bouncing against the ground. The resentment and hatred were fading away. Galina felt as if she had recovered from a bad, exhausting illness. She could breathe again, she could look at Raya, she could talk to her again.

Galina got out of the tramcar. She didn't know where she wanted to go. She thought of turning right and continuing to walk on tree-lined Chkalov Street, and she even took a few steps in that direction, but something made her change her mind and continue walking along the tramline, toward city hall. The street ran down the hill; it was easier to walk and Galina walked faster.

Was there a single moment when this present chilliness between her and Raya had started? Now it seemed that their relationship wasn't descending smoothly, but lurching downward by tugs the way a rusty old elevator does. A lurch—a stop—a lurch—a stop.

The first lurch happened because of that ridiculous business of praying for their husbands. There had been no news or letters from the front. The girls asked questions at first, but then they stopped. They understood. They didn't mention their fathers, and if they did, accidentally, they immediately stopped and exchanged panicky looks, as if they thought that the lives of their fathers were so fragile right now that anything, even saying their names aloud, could destroy them. Galina and Raya did not mention their husbands either. They agreed that the subject would be too upsetting. But Galina wondered if the true reason for their silence was the fear of insincerity.

The prayers had been started by the girls. Galina didn't know who had the idea, Tanya or Leeza. Neither of them knew how to pray. They had never been in church and never heard anyone pray at home. Their pleas sounded more like Christmas wishes: "Kind, dear God, please, don't let my father die." For a few evenings, Galina and Raya just watched the girls. They watched their little bodies rocking softly, while their mouths eagerly breathed out naïve words of prayer. Their eyes were directed somewhere upward, as if there, on Galina's white-washed ceiling, was the figure of God, visible only to them.

One evening, after the girls had gone to sleep, Raya suggested that she and Galina pray, too. She looked embarrassed when she said it. She was playing with the fringe on the tablecloth and avoided looking at Galina. Raya said that she didn't believe in God and didn't know how to pray, but maybe it would make her feel better. Galina shrugged. They got down on their knees, making the rough floor-boards creak, and stayed in these awkward poses, not knowing what to say. Raya was the first to begin; she started the way the girls did. "Dear God . . ." Galina had often heard her mother pray, and she'd even been in church with her once or twice, but she couldn't remember any words—just "Amen," which her mother used at the end, before she got up from her knees, groaning and crossing herself. Galina had to fill the gap between "Dear God" and "Amen" somehow. She tried to invoke warm feelings about her husband, but instead she caught herself blaming him. She thought that it was his fault that they had stayed in the town. It was his fault that he'd been kicked out of the Party. "Engaged in inappropriate behavior! Some rebel!" Galina thought. She knew that he had simply showed up drunk at one of the Party committee meetings and that it wasn't the first time. She remembered how he spent all their money on vodka. She remembered how, when he couldn't find the money, he took things from home and sold them at the flea market. He sold Galina's favorite lamp, the one with a blue velvet shade. She tried harder to find some forgiveness. She tried to think about Sergey the way Tanya did. Tanya, who always rushed to her father when he came home drunk, helped him to undress, stroked his puffy, apologetic face, and said, when he slipped and fell, "It's okay, Daddy, the floor is slippery. We just washed it." How could Tanya treat him this way, when it was the money for her coat that he stole and spent? He would come back from the front and steal more money, and they would have to continue living like that. Galina felt bitter, angry tears coming up her throat. Could it be that she didn't want Sergey to come back? Could it be that she wanted him to die? The thought startled her. She felt her heart pounding heavily against her rib cage, hurting her, as if it were made of stone. She turned to look at Raya. She was kneeling with her head bent low. Her tightly shut eyelids were trembling, her chapped lips moving eagerly; she licked them with a swift movement from time to time. Galina watched her, feeling that her own guilt was fading, making a place for her resentment of Raya: "Some faithful little wife!"

The next night, Galina said that she didn't feel like praying. So they didn't do it again. And soon their prewar recollections stopped, too. That was when Raya began writing letters to her husband every night. Just a few tortured lines, with words crossed out, written over, then crossed out again. She often turned to glance in Galina's direction, and it was then that her expression became frightened. But they were still talking. Not as much as before and not as easily, but not yet the complete silence of recent weeks.

Galina felt that something sharp was in her right boot. It was rolling under her foot, hurting her when she occasionally stepped on it. She limped to a lamppost. There she leaned on the cold concrete pole and removed her boot, reaching with her hand into the boot's warm, damp inside to pull out a tiny jagged rock. It must have been a piece of gravel from her walk along the rails. She pulled the boot back on and moved her numbed toes.

She knew why they had stopped talking. It was because of Raya's earrings. Galina could close her eyes and see them now. They were the most beautiful things she had ever seen. Small, elongated pieces of turquoise, shaped like large raindrops, hanging on thin golden threads with tiny curved golden petals connecting the turquoise drop to the thread. Raya used to wear them every day, even with the clothes that didn't match their exquisite blue color. She said that without the earrings she looked naked. "And ugly, and old," she added, laughing. She had taken them off that night when she and Leeza were supposed to leave town with the peasant. And it was true that without them Raya's face looked naked and drawn of color. Without the earrings, Galina could see that Raya's pale skin had a grayish tone and that her ears were too big for her face. Galina wondered what had happened to the earrings—had Raya hidden them somewhere, or did she have them with her. Until the day she saw them again.

It happened a few days after their attempt at praying. Raya came out of the back room with a tiny bundle, something gray and fuzzy. She was holding it carefully on her outstretched palm as if it were a baby bird. When she got closer to Galina, Galina saw that it was not a bundle but an old woolen mitten. Raya reached inside and pulled out a faded matchbox. Galina guessed what was inside before Raya opened it, but still, seeing the earrings in all their brilliance here, against the shabby surface of the matchbox, was shocking. Galina could see that it was shocking to Raya, too. They stared at the earrings for a few seconds, then Raya said, stretching her lips into a smile: "I thought maybe you could exchange them for milk? Or cream? Leeza's cough has been bad lately." She touched the earrings, running her translucent fingers along the thin veins in the turquoise. "It's light turquoise and gold—they used to be expensive."

So Galina took them to their little town market. She carried them the same way, in a matchbox wrapped in the mitten. She squeezed past rows of peasant women in long, thick skirts and gray shawls. They were holding bushels of eggs with dried-up chicken droppings stuck to them, coarse gray loaves of bread, and shriveled potatoes. They had sleek faces and shrewd little eyes. And there were rows of women in urban clothes with pitiful pieces of jewelry dangling in their pale fingers. Earrings, cheap necklaces, thin wedding rings, men's watches. These women had long faces and desperate, begging eyes. Galina passed them quickly and went to the end of the row, where she often saw a farmer woman selling milk. There she was, a short woman with a fat, oily face under a filthy headscarf. There were two big aluminum milk cans by her feet and a clay jar covered with a piece of cloth in her hands. "Cream," said the woman to Galina in an intimate whisper. Galina looked at the woman's hands; she had cut-off woolen gloves on, and her fingers were fat and red, with dirt under the fingernails. Galina imagined Raya's earrings in these hands, and how the woman would try to fasten them with her swollen fingers. Then she imagined the earrings dangling on their golden threads next to the woman's greasy cheeks. She knew it was unlikely that the woman would wear the earrings herself; she would probably wait for better times and sell them, but still she felt that she wouldn't be able to bear seeing the earrings in the woman's hands even during the brief moment of transaction. She put her hand into her coat pocket and pushed the mitten with the earrings further down. She acquired the jar of cream in exchange for a bar of soap that she carried in her other pocket.

As she walked back from the market, Galina knew that she wouldn't tell Raya about the earrings. She would tell her that she had sold them. She would come home and hide them in her drawer between stacks of her flannel sheets. There was one woman on the market selling a mirror. Galina stopped there, unwrapped the package quickly and held the earrings against her ears. She was in such a hurry to wrap them back up that she only saw a glimpse of her reflection, her rigid face instantly brightened by two light-blue spots. All the way home, Galina told herself that she hadn't done anything wrong. After all, Raya and Leeza ate her supplies of food. And they lived at her home. And she had paid for the cream with her bar of soap. The earrings were a small price. She had the right to them. Galina kept fingering the package all the way home. Every time she touched the soft, fuzzy surface of the mitten and the hard edge of the matchbox underneath, she felt a thrill, a titillating feeling of getting away with something.

Her elevated mood vanished as soon as she saw Raya's face. As soon as she saw that Raya knew. Raya rushed to the jar of cream, showering Galina with praises, repeating that the cream would save Leeza's life, displaying exaggerated gratitude to the point where it began making Galina dizzy. Raya's behavior was made up of two strands, contradictory and sickening. The first was to show that she never, not for a moment, could suppose that Galina hadn't sold the earrings. The second was to show that if Galina did take the earrings, Raya didn't mind; on the contrary, she was happy that Galina might have done that, it was Galina's right to do that, Galina risked her life for them and the earrings were such a small price. Galina went to the kitchen, pretending that she had things to do there. She began scrubbing the pots that she hadn't used in months with her trembling hands. If only Raya would shut up!

Later that day, Galina came to a realization. She watched how Raya tried to feed the warmed-up cream to Leeza. "Please, darling, please, it'll make you feel better." Leeza swallowed it spoon by spoon, slowly, reluctantly. At one moment she choked and began coughing, and Raya patted her on the back, while throwing a nervous glance in Galina's direction. She wanted Galina to take the earrings! Maybe she had even made it all up—made up the whole story about milk for Leeza—to make Galina take the earrings. Galina felt a heavy, cold wave of nausea. She had to grab a doorframe to keep her balance. Raya wanted to bribe her. Galina went back to the kitchen and sank down on the low stool. She wanted to bribe her! Why? Because she was afraid that Galina would ask her to go? Or worse, because she was afraid that Galina would walk downtown and tell the Germans that there were Jews in her house. No, that was ridiculous, the Germans would kill her and Tanya if they knew that they were giving shelter to Jews. Or would they? She could always say that they had been hiding somewhere else, that they had just come to her place to ask for shelter or for food, and she immediately went to report it. Nobody would be interested in finding out the truth, and nobody there would listen to Raya. These thoughts startled Galina. What was happening? Was she just trying to unravel Raya's way of thinking, or was she really considering going to the Germans? She took a cold teakettle off the stove and began drinking hungrily right out of its rough tin spout. The streams of water ran down her chin and her neck, causing her skin to break out in goose bumps.

The tramline made a sharp turn on the crossing. It was the first time since the beginning of the occupation that Galina had gone so far downtown. It had gotten considerably darker since she left the house; soon she would have to turn back to make it home before curfew. Or she could walk the last two or three blocks toward city hall. Lately, whenever she went to the market, which was not so far from downtown, she had the urge to turn in the city hall direction. She couldn't understand what it was that attracted her to that place.

Galina had no desire to see the Germans. She despised all those women who rushed to the center in the first days of occupation to see what Germans looked like. They even looked up some German words in a dictionary so they would be able to introduce themselves. Galina saw one girl from the library, a freckled Masha, bending over a German phrasebook and repeating over and over, *"Ich heisse Mascha,"* her thin lips making a funny circle when she said *"Ich."*

Galina wondered how much German she remembered. She had good grades in high school, but it had been more than ten years since she'd held a German textbook in her hands. *"Hier ist ein Tisch." "Das Wetter ist schön heute."* It was strange how these expressions, buried in her memory for so many years, were now coming to surface. Galina made another effort. *"Gretchen geht nach Schule."* She smiled. German words were rolling under her tongue like sucking candies. She tried to apply some of the expressions to herself. *"Ich heisse Galina"; "Galina geht nach Schule."* She wondered if her lips looked as funny as Masha's. How did they say "How are you"? *"Ich geht . . ."* No, no . . . *"Wie geht es Ihnen?"* Something like that.

Galina forgot about her tired, aching legs. She walked briskly to the brightly lit city hall plaza. The German words were floating up in her head one after another, forming sentences and whole conversations:

Hello. *Wie geht es Ihnen?*
Danke gut. Und ihnen?
Danke auch gut. Ich heisse Galina. Es gibt Juden in mein Haus.

Galina's heart skipped a beat, then began pounding wildly. She took off her headscarf and unbuttoned her jacket. *Es gibt Juden in mein Haus. Es gibt Juden in mein Haus. Es gibt Juden in mein Haus.* The words seemed glued to her lips. They were burning her, scorching the inside of her mouth and further down her throat. She didn't really want to say those words. She couldn't. But what if she could? Galina saw that she was very close to the city hall plaza now. She could see lights coming from the shabby brick building of the former city hall. She could see German vehicles. She could hear the whirring of motors. If she took just a few more steps, she would have been able to hear real German speech, not just the textbook variations.

Galina turned around and started running in the opposite direction. She ran very fast, as if the Germans were chasing her, her white headscarf streaming in the wind like a flag. She couldn't want to do that. It wasn't true. It was all because of Raya! Raya had pushed her. Raya was distrustful and ungrateful. Raya would have never done for Galina what Galina was doing for her. Galina was a good person. She was risking her own and her daughter's life to save Raya and Leeza. Galina felt that she couldn't run anymore, she was out of breath. Somehow words about risking her life never moved her. She couldn't make herself feel that she was doing something heroic. Maybe that was because she didn't feel fear. She knew how dangerous it was to hide Jews in her house; she knew that there was a war going on and that people in occupied towns could be killed for lesser crimes; but something prevented her from imagining that she or Tanya could be killed or even hurt. And she couldn't fear anything that she couldn't vividly imagine. She wished that she could.

Their staircase was completely dark, and Galina had to fumble with her hand on the wall to find the door. She hoped that Raya wouldn't come out of her room. If Raya saw Galina's face, she would guess her thoughts, the same way she knew about the earrings. She would know about *"Es gibt Juden in mein Haus."* Galina knocked on the wooden frame four times before opening the door with her key. Raya had asked Galina to do that.

It was very quiet inside. There was only Tanya in the room playing with her doll at the table. The door of the back room was closed. "They're sleeping," Galina thought with relief and went to the sink to wash the mud off her boots. Only when she came out of the bathroom did Galina notice Tanya's blank stare and that she wasn't playing with the doll but simply holding it in her hands, upside down. "Why are you not in bed? Are they sleeping?" Galina asked. Tanya shook her head. "They're gone," she said. Galina walked to the table, the dripping boots still clutched in her hands. The foolish, irrational questions were pouring out of her mouth: "What do you mean 'gone'? Where? When did they leave? Why do you have the doll? Did they say anything?" Then she heard herself screaming: "What do you mean 'gone'?!" Tanya walked to her bed and began undressing. She spoke in an odd, tired voice: "They got dressed and left right after you left. Leeza said she wouldn't need the doll anymore." Tanya paused. "What did she mean? What did Aunt Raya say? Did Raya say anything? Why wouldn't Leeza need the doll?"

Tanya stood by the bed in her white underpants and white undershirt, silently folding her clothes. Then she put her dress on a chair, her ribbed brown tights on top of it, and turned off the light.

Galina slumped on a chair in the dark and sat listening to the creaking of Tanya's wooden bed as she climbed in, to the rustle of the sheets, to Tanya's long, muffled sobbing—she must have had a pillow over her head—and then to the sounds of her breathing gradually getting soft and quiet. Galina thought of the questions that Tanya couldn't stop asking before Raya and Leeza came to live with them. "How do they catch Jews? Do they chase them? Do they use ropes? Does it hurt when they burn them? Do they become all black and shriveled like burned firewood? Does it hurt a lot?"

Galina stood up and tiptoed to Tanya's bed. The pillow was still on her head. Galina gently lifted up her head and put the pillow under it. She looked at Tanya's shoulders—strong tanned shoulders, so much like her own. Galina looked at the round white scar on Tanya's upper arm, just below her shoulder bone. She reached out with her hand and stroked her daughter awkwardly. Tanya flinched in her sleep and pulled her shoulder under the blanket. Galina tiptoed away from the bed. She stumbled on something by the table. Something that made her heart stop beating. Something cold, both hard and soft, with hair. "A dead child," the thought flashed in Galina's head. She couldn't breathe, she couldn't bring herself to look down, she couldn't move her foot.

Then she looked down and saw the contours of Leeza's doll, barely visible in the dark.